PLANET SALV

by Joshua Seraphim

PLANET SALV

Leilah Publications

To order wholesale, please contact:
American Wholesale Book Company (205) 956-4151
Ingram Book Company (800) 937-8000
Baker & Taylor (800) 775-1100

Leilah Publications P.O. Box 1863 Tempe, AZ 85280
U.S.A.

Leilah Publications brings a global vision of art & writing for the 21st century, publishing & investing in avante-garde artists, writers, and visionaries. The company was founded in 2006 to publish the visions of prodigies, leading us into the 21st century under a new generation of visionary artists, lyricists, writers, actors & actresses, and poets.

Deepest gratitude to the master Artists Stefan Wul, René Laloux, and Roland Topor for giving us their masterpiece "The Fantastic Planet." Their vision lives on and can never be replicated, duplicated, or remade....

TABLE OF CONTENTS

PLANET SALV

Night was somnolent blue on the Fantastic Planet of the Draags...a single iridescent red mediation sphere arose and drifted...

I.   PLANET SALV

Outside the dimensions of the First Generation galaxies, a titanic Seazoytezeem whale swallowed a nebula whole. Stars went nova when in range of the Seazoytezeem whale's singing. Resembling a Terran ocean whale on a titanic scale, the Seazoytezeem whale giggled and sang as it swam through the stellar expanse.

When the savage human species was in utero within the great Sleeper, twelve species on the elder worlds were chosen to cultivate the spiral galaxies and elliptical nebulas. Atomic subconscious fused with chimerical visions of fantastic species. Alien meditations dissolved into radial dimensions. Galaxies, stars, and nebulas spiraled into existence from the vaporous breathing of the titanic Whales of the Seazoytezeem worlds. The Salvs were known to many races in the First Generation galaxies as "The Sleepers," for only a few beings knew the secret of how long the Salvs slept, or why.

Only a small group of Quantum-warping races in the First Generation galaxies, and the Ancient Artisans who constructed the nebula sized wormhole conduits used by millions of Quantum-warping races knew the secret of the Salv Sleep. The Artisans could raise entire empires with words; their psi-chanting could shatter planets, even the vapor emitting each moment of corporeal touch between two Artisans became nebulas, quasars, and vast pulsars.

The world-sized crystalline spiders of the Circinus galaxy dissolved the mathematical impossibilities in physics from human brainwaves. The human Milky Way oozed into spiral transformation from the luminescent sensual vapors of the Salvs emitted during their fantastic sexual rites. The cosmic vapors emitted by the Artisans and their distant Salv cousins formed over millions of years and light years the empyrean expanse. With their extraordinary metaphysical psionic force, the Salvs could regenerate atoms and protons into dark matter, forming the building blocks of new galaxies and stars. For the Salvs, and the Artisans of the First Generation galaxies, the cosmos was a garden to be cultivated and harvested.

Species from myriads of galaxies traveled through warped space just to witness the strange concupiscent rites of the Salvs. Salv meditations and visions were ethereal and luminous, unlike anything, any species in the First Generation Galaxies ever observed. The concupiscent rites between two Salvs lasted the equivalent of three Terran orbits around its pale red star. Continuous transcendence.

The Salvine expression of physical desire transcended lower-evolutionary sex impulses. Fervent Salvine conjunctions merged the consciousness and physical form of two Salv mates into a singular Being, synchronizing their super-evolved minds with the living universe. Three stages of erotic convergence occurred, in elegant synchronicity of telepathic consciousness.

The first period of the Salvic rite involved their two tentacles, called *divis*, ritually dancing and sliding along each of their bodies. Shimmering spots, small and numerous along a Salv's body glowed. Vaporous mists fumed from their *divi* tentacles, cascading around the planet giving it a bio-luminescent glow. The Salv mating mists exuded from the concupiscent ritual out from the atmosphere and into the cosmos in a nebulous blue radiance.

Chimerical meditations on erotic convergence of consciousness between two Salvs expanded until the two Salvs morphed physically into one luminous being. This was the fantastic second period of the Rite. Visiting species came to enlightened expansion of consciousness in the presence of this metamorphic sensuality.

Climaxes of the concupiscent rites transformed the consciousness of the Salv-hybrid into an explosive life force. A molecular eruption that forms stars and nebulas. Sexual orgasm occurred *only when the two beings separated*. Meditation allowed the two mating Salvs transference of consciousness to any beings in the First Generation Galaxies.

The more beings receiving consciousness-transference from a Salv, the greater the orgasm. A luminescent blue radiance encased the entire planet informed other species and spectators of orgasmic climax. If the two Salvs remained in physical contact after the first period, physical death befell each of the mating Salvs.

An adult humanoid Salv reached up to a hundred meters high. Deep red and indigo in skin tone, shimmering dusts of light glowed in fantastic displays along the skin. Two lidless large penetrating golden eyes spiraled and reflected the starry cosmos during their chimerical meditations, and concupiscent rites. Salv *divi* tentacles hung the length of their bodies where auditory lobes would be on many humanoid species. *Divis* performed the function of sex organs and all sensory perceptions. Salvs chose not engage in vocal speech, communicating clairvoyantly.

Salvs were the most attractive and ethereal species in the First Generation Galaxies. On all the worlds in the First Generation Galaxies, the Salvs were the most sought after species an elite quantum-warping family of races because of their philosophic and psionic knowledge. In this elite group, among the few species that shared consciousness transference with the Salvs were; the Nepetoid spider-cetaceans, the enormous philosopher wooly-mammoths of Nod, the sun-eating solar dragons in Andromeda, the ancient feline races of Juul, and the Draags of Ygam.

Where is Planet Salv? Far beyond the farthest star you can see. Along the innermost Rim of Hoag's Object, an atypical ring galaxy, 600 million light years away in the constellation Serpens; a pale blue star illuminates the stellar expanse…a lone indigo sparkle hangs in the deep void, as the jewel of the First Generation galaxies. Here, asleep for an unknown time, are the Salvs.

Planet Salv was an indigo sparkle in a far corner of the first generation galaxies. Salv's indigo sparkle reflected its blue star off the planet's outer Febula rings, casting a reflective violet glow about the planet's atmosphere at nightfall. Salv had no natural satellite. Salv's sister world, which they called the "Lost Planet" hung low and radiant on the Salv horizon, never changing. The "Lost Planet" never moved. The timeless intruder in the Salvine sky had no natural orbit of its own.

Salv story-oracles told their young about the Lost Planet's appearance, or invasion, long ago on their horizon. One day when their world was still populated by the Great Golams before the Convergence of the Salv Tribes, all Salvs looked up to a bright light over the evening horizon. Their "Lost Planet" artlessly appeared one day in the dawn of Salvic recorded time. It never moved, it never grew dim or brighter. No Salv had ever set foot on the strange planet. To do so, Salvs believed, was sacrilege.

Salvs shared their fantastic planet with the Opians. Co-habitation on Planet Salv was a unique situation for both races, each remained aware of the other's respective existence and domain. Opian brains were not as developed biologically on the evolutionary scale as their Salvic cousins. Ranging several meters shorter than the average-sized Salv, Opians were also humanoid bipeds, like Salvs. Opian skin hues ranged from light to darker shades of green. A minority percentage of Opians were light green skinned with blue highlights in contrast to the deep red and violet Salv skin tones.

These slightly different toned Opians were higher in social strata in Opiate society than the regular greens. Only the greens with blue highlights were permitted on the exclusive Council that governed the rest of the Opian tribes. The blue-green administrators, Opians called *Lums* governed Opiate society under the *"Luminist Council."* All Opians were deferential to Luminist proclamations.

Opian and Salv societies had an unusual coexistence, each aware of the other's civilization and levels of evolution. Opian society was reclusive and had little contact with the Salvs; their culture was xenophobic yet voyeuristic concerning their Salv cousins. Opians ranged up to several meters shorter than any Salv, both were bipedal, and humanoid, yet the Salvs possessed a sort of fluid glide in their movement due to the low gravity on their planet. Opians sauntered and scurried often quickly and held their upper bodies and head down as if in deference to Salvs they might encounter.

Opians had large lidless red eyes adding to the characteristic of a shy curiosity to Opian facial structure and their gait. Like their Salv cousins, the Opians were hairless and had two shorter *divi* tentacles hanging a quarter the length of their bodies where auditory lobes would be on many humanoid species. Their shorter *divis* performed the function of sex organs and all Opian sensory perceptions. Though not as different physically and biologically, Opians spoke vocally and had natural births resulting from sexual intercourse. Artificial biodomes , smaller than Salvic biodomes, served as dwellings for hundreds of tribal affiliated Opians, each further broken down into *toolas*, or familial units.

Opian society lived in xenophobic suspicion of Salvs. Salvs understood the Opian language and could telepathically project it fluently; learning the intricate overlying Opian dialects and cacophonic chanting-like sibilant speech through their telepathic transference with Opians. Opians were required to learn the unspoken ancient language of the Salvs in their formal learning centers. Opians had never heard the Salvic language spoken audibly save for their own use of the dead language in religious rites to the Lost Planet.

The Opian *Luminist Council* convened every three Salvic alignments (an period on Salv measured by Lums and Salvs lasting three Terran months) to administrate agricultural, scientific, and infrastructure utility programs. Numerous Opian space rockets, powered by rudimentary nuclear propulsion, reached orbit around the Lost Planet and deployed satellites to study it but never landed any probes on the surface. Opians believed the entire planet was supernatural and conducted religious rites to placate what they believed to be the spirits of deceased Opians and Salvs that traveled to the Lost Planet after death.

Data about the Lost Planet transmitted back to Opian scientists was inconclusive and unusable. Opian scientists distinguished no weather patterns, climate signatures, geological composition, or any information about the strange object. Satellites calculated the Lost Planet's mean radius at 3,914 kilometres, slightly larger than Terra's solar neighbor Mars. Opian rocket ships carried their scientists into orbit around Salv for the past 20 conjunctions (several Terran decades). Vehement debate increased in the Luminist Council over whether Opian scientists should attempt a landing on the Lost Planet.

It would only be another conjunction before Opians believed their rockets would be equipped with new propulsion technology that would allow them interplanetary travel to nearby planets in the Salvine star system. Although Salv was the only inhabited planet in their star system, the Opians longed to mine the rare minerals and gases detected by their satellites on their planetary neighbors. Debate over landing Opians on the Lost Planet raged in the Luminist Council and gradually began to divide Opian tribes with their religious leaders strongly denouncing any landing on the Lost Planet, while the scientists successfully convinced many Opian tribal councils that landing on the Lost Planet could unlock secrets to their mysterious Salv cousins.

Opians believed the Salvs were mystic, and evasive. The two races seldom encountered one another; Salvic days could turn into weeks and months without Opians seeing a Salv. Opians rarely attempted to communicate with a Salv, when the rare encounter occurred. The cautious Opians would usually bow their heads or shuffle away hurriedly while the Salv would stand and observe silently. Opians were not as developed psychically as Salvs, many Opian Lums possessed the ability of telepathy or extra-sensory perception and could sense when a Salv attempted to converge with their minds.

It was rare for a Salv to engage in convergence with an Opian's conscious mind, yet some Opians reported different experiences resulting from mindshifting. Many Opians became terrified when they felt a Salv mindshift eclipse their subconsciousness with superior knowledge that spanned tens of thousands of years of spiritual and psychic development. Other Opians found the mindshift spiritual and transcendent, nearly all reported varying levels of lasting physical stimulation. A silent minority of Opian Lums found the Salv mindshifts sexually stimulating. Opian healers reported rare cases of nerve-injury, and in extreme cases, death.

Psilocybes glided noisily across the Salvine sky, their long snouts snorting and chirping, at each other, unaware of hungry cephalopods called Peyotoids hovering patiently above. As the Peyotoids devoured their unsuspecting tasty prey, iridescent red Daturyte plants gurgled and chortled while towering psilozoyte plants fluttered and flapped. Sentient plant life swayed raucously while Salvic beasts crawled, floated, and hovered, all emitting sounds that would astonish human ears. Glowing mists floated beneath the indigo Salv horizon.

A male and female Opian walked down the esplanade of their Vil. Juuri, the taller female spoke quietly. "I had the dreams again Kwai. They were so real." Kwai, the shorter male Opian, curled his divis. "Dreams? About the pyramid monoliths again?" "Yes." Juuri replied. "I was other Lums. We were watching the monoliths, waiting for something Kwai. Then…then they began to change." "Change? How" Kwai asked, curling his divis apprehensively. Juuri's divis also twitched as she continued. "I do not know. They just….changed. I cannot explain it Kwai. It was so real." "I do not even like to look at them. They scare me Juuri. It is as if…as if the Sleepers are not sleeping at all, but waiting." The two Opians continued along the esplanade silently.

II.   THE DRAAGS AFTER TERR

Millions of light years away, radiant red meditation spheres floated and drifted into the skies of Ygam, the Draag homeworld. It had been nearly a generation since the Era of Sinh, the period of the Masters of Ygam. Tiva was now a fully matured adult Draag. She had come to hypothesize about her and her father's role in the great peace between the Oms and Draags, facilitated by the Council led by her father, Master Sinh and her former domesticated Om, Terr.

It was the whirling reality of the Great Zarek that had shifted such a great evolutionary change in Draag civilization, Tiva realized. She never saw Terr again after he left with her info bracelet when she was still a Draag child. Father and Mother had forbidden her to meet with any Om until the relocation of nearly all the Oms to their artificial satellite, Terra. By then Terr had lived out his human lifespan as Tiva matured into an adult Draag.

Tiva was not thinking of the Oms, nor were her meditations on the Oms or the dynamic evolutionary changes in Draag civilization. For several seasons now, Tiva and her compatriot's chimerical melding meditations were vivid, and yet troubling. Tiva sat in meditation with her compatriots, their spirits encased by glowing red spheres. The radiant red spheres rose high above their Uva into the skies of Ygam, drifting towards the Fantastic Planet. For what was about to occur on the Fantastic Planet were strange nuptial rites, and the fate of the First Generation galaxies would change forever.

III.   LATTICES OF LIGHT

They were called The Artisans. Not remotely human, they were the one of the first species to evolve and be able to quantum-warp the space-time continuum. In the entire universe and its secrets from the stars, The Artisans found nothing more precious than Mind. Biological forms of flesh and blood, they evolved over thousands of years and explored their neighboring planets while the Milky Way and Andromeda were not yet formed in the cosmic pool of light. The Artisans sought for fellowship among the stars, evolving past the need for biological bodies ten thousand years after their first orbital launch of an artificial satellite. The tides of civilization ebbed and fluctuated across the First Generation galaxies.

The Artisans saw strange, majestic, and terrible empires rise and fall. When technology merged and transcended their biological forms, The Artisans reached a development of spiritual singularity, transferring first their brains, then their consciousness to shining crystalline sentient ships of matter and light. It became time for the Artisans to move. In these they roamed the universe and learned to create a causal vortex and quantum-warp through time.

The Artisans became the masters of time and space, creating the Great Conduits that other fellowships and empires of interstellar species would utilize to cross galaxies. In their ceaseless quantum experiments, The Artisans learned to store their knowledge among the stars in moving lattices of light. Like living mists they roamed time and space, becoming free from the tyranny of matter. Few species triggered direct intervention in the manifest destiny of their evolutionary scale by The Artisans.

One million years ago, The Artisans saved the serpentine Vinithii race from certain extinction at the hands of terrible time-warpers called the Syntinnid; a horrific race that could quantum-warp time-space, and had annihilated and enslaved thousands of galaxies, millions of species. The Syntinnid fed off the psychic brainwaves of species and could consume biological life forms in a suspended state, keeping their prey alive in unspeakable suffering. The insectoid xenomorph Syntinnid were one of the most feared and terrible species in the universe. The Artisans saved the Vinithii from extinction at the hands of the Syntinnid. Centuries later, the Vinithii along with the Salvs, and a few other species founded a benevolent fellowship that spanned a dozen galaxies.

The Vinithii and Salvs long evolved past the need for formal cultural fellowship among space-warping species. The Fellowship passed its knowledge and culture on to its successors. The Great Sleep of the Salvs was one of the unexpected and extraordinary instances where The Artisans intervened to save the Salvs from extinction. Unknown to the Salvs, The Artisans foresaw through time, numerous causal streams that led to Salv extinction or ruin. Thousands of conjunctions ago on Salv, long before the Great Convergence of the Salv tribes, when the Great Golams still roamed the landscape, the Artisans placed inverted Floating Pyramid Monoliths in a remote location.

Salv tribes soon discovered the extraordinary floating pyramids, which became a sacred site where the Salv tribes all sang the Soliloquy of Convergence. The inverted Floating Monolith Pyramids of Salv became their most sacred site, after the Lost Planet. Salvs believed their meditative and religious use of the upside-down Floating Monoliths led to the appearance of the Lost Planet in their skies.

While they learned to farm and harvest the deep void, the Salvs used the Great Conduits built by the Artisans. The large red and indigo humanoids with their concupiscent rites lasting several Terran years came to uncover the secrets of the floating inverted Pyramids. They also discovered a possible connection to the Lost World.

IV.   THE LOST PLANET

When the Salvs looked out across the deeps of space, they wondered in awe, marveled at its secrets – and they felt loneliness. They watched the waking of evolution and spiritual crucible as intelligent life-forms in all their beauty floated, crawled, flew, and walked; all lifting their gaze to the deeps of space. The Salvs reached an extraordinary crucible. Peace shattered across two worlds; conjoining unexpectedly the destinies of four races. The Lost World carried its secret from the stars. The Floating Pyramid Monoliths, glowed radiant indigo. The Sleeping Salvs remained latent within them.

Will we dream Zsiji? Sapia, a young maturing Salv, telepathically voiced her sister and mate. "Yes." Zsiji answered. "We will dream." Until they awakened, the trustees of the stars did not know that the stars seen in their dreams did not exist. Stars fell around the Salvs. Minds reflected the deeps of space in violent loneliness. The Sleepers dreamt while The Artisans watched. *When the Trinity of the Watchers aligns in the skies of Salv, the Great Sleep will end...the floating Pyramids will upturn blackened as the cosmic night.* This was the Salv Prophecy foretold by the Salv oracle Zejiss at the Third Soliloquy of Convergence. The trustees of the stars awakened.

Inside the floating inverted monoliths, the latent Salvs lay encapsulated in a cocoon of fluidic white luminescence, which dimmed and dissipated as the Salvs awakened. Subconsciousness slipped into whirling reality as Sapia slowly opened her golden eyes. Psionic scans of her physiology revealed her body was quickly overcoming lasting effects of stasis and dystrophy. She could concentrate and regenerate the molecular cellular structure of her tissue within minutes; yet Sapia required all her psionic faculties in the Awakening.

The white luminescent cocoon dimmed around the surviving Salvs. Peering over to Zsiji's cocoon, Sapia could see the concern on her psi-mate's face as she regenerated damaged internal nervous systems. How many of them survived? Sapia could feel her psi-mates disquieting thoughts. Zsiji and Sapia slowly arose as white fluidic luminescence continued to dim and dissipate in succession, signifying awakening Salvs.

The luminous red and indigo floating Pyramids shuddered and slowly upturned. The floating monoliths now were proper crimson pyramids, shimmering red and indigo fluidic light. Slowly the luminous monoliths lost their light, dimming at first to a dull crimson, then turning hazy and opaque, finally to black. The Salvs inside quietly began to chant, first telepathically then as the psionic bond amplified, their psionic vital-force became aural. Harmonic conjunction lifted their chanting, echoing inside their monolithic Pyramids. Floating while suspended in the air, the blackened Pyramids numbered three, resembling solemn death markers.

Inside the suspended black pyramids, the Salv chanting stopped. For many Salvs it was the first time they ever heard their own aural voices. Zsiji and Sapia moved toward the far wall of the Pyramid while the others telepathically voiced each other or reflected on hearing their own voices for the first time. Zsiji and Salv looked into each other's eyes, bonding telepathically as psi-mates. The two Salvs allowed the vital-force to flow into their divis, slowly sliding them and gyrating along each other.

Zsiji silently gave Sapia her affirmation within the telepathic bond. Sapia touched rhythmically a series of small oblong shapes near the centre of the far wall. A series of small glowing white lines appeared in succession and grew larger, creating geometric patterns the size of Salvs themselves. Sapia turned with Zsiji, their divis still undulating and intertwining slowly. She allowed her telepathic bond with Zsiji to encase each of the minds around her; feeling their thoughts and sensations. Each Salv reciprocated the psionic alignment, soon each felt the others neural pathways and pulsing divis.

Sapia spoke aurally; her melodic voice sang and resonated within the artificial Pyramids. *Precious ones, the Great Sleep has ended. We are trustees to the stars; let us create a new alignment, as farmers in the fields of stars. Let us regenerate a new harvest and cultivate the breathing living deeps of space. We are patient but not immortal, we have so much to learn and harvest in this universe of a hundred billion galaxies, other beings sing to us, the stars sang to us as we slept. Let us return the song.* Salvs began to chant telepathically and aurally reinforcing Zsiji and Sapia's psionic bond. Their vital-force caused glowing red mists to emit from their divis, morphing into radiant meditation spheres.

The luminous red meditation spheres encased each chanting Salv, as their divis undulated and curled in harmonic conjunction. The Salv meditation spheres rose and hovered through the illuminated white geometric patterns on the blackened far wall. Setting down on the ground beneath the suspended Pyramids, the spheres dissipated as each Salv stepped out from within. Zsiji and Sapia looked at each other. The Salvs in their Pyramid were the only survivors. Sapia stood up from the meditation sphere and walked a few meters along the terrain of the Lost Planet.

...

V.   SETI AND TURA

Opians and Salvs co-habited their homeworld before the Great Sleep of the Salvs. Uncommon encounters between Opian and Salv were strange, mesmerizing Opians who chanced upon a strange Salv. Encounters between the two races often spanned many alignments. Stories of an Opian chancing upon the strange Salv would spread rapidly among the toolas, and soon the entire tribe would know of the bizarre occurrence. Eluding the Salv when seeing one in proximity was the preferred action by Opians.   Rarely did a Salv ever approach an Opian. When a Salv did initiate contact, the Salv stood a few meters away, tilting its head side to side; slowly curling and uncoiling their divis as a sign of passive communication.

Salvs choosing to interact with their Opian cousins looked directly into their eyes, adjoining their thoughts and psychological sensations. Minimal transference followed Salv consciousness inflowing to conjoin Opian brainwaves. Two minds became one, confusing the Opian contactee, engulfing their mind in euphoric trance.

Opians who experienced the Salv mindshift remained in a state of physical euphoria for days, others became catatonic. Small numbers of Opian Lums, who endured the fantastic mindshifts, became highly religious, some abandoning their toolas and daily labours, leaving their biosphere to seek a life of philosophic contemplation and meditation in Salv biospheres.

Seti, a young female Opian who was the daughter of Master Junal in the Luminist Council strolled with her male compatriot, Tura through one of their numerous scientific amphitheaters. As they passed the amphitheater, the two Opians caught sight of an artificial Salv biodome. Tura coiled and uncoiled his divis apprehensively. "Salvs. They never speak to us...they never speak at all to us...they never come out and when they do it is only to address the Lums! We cannot even plant a Searine garden without them knowing about it, Seti!" Seti looked at her companion, undulating her divi tentacles. "Tura, have they ever mindshifted with you?" She asked the older Opian. "Yes Seti, it was something I never want to experience again I was vertiginous for days...I am afraid to meditate now. Did you know Salvis sense our meditations and even our dreams? And they always show up in Councils when the Lums plan a satellite launch." Seti's divis twitched around her in disdain.

The two Opians continued talking unaware of a dark red-skinned humanoid, a few meters taller than them, standing behind them quietly watching. "Why do the Lums give them almost all our Searine crops, just so they can make their Spice?" Seti was speaking as the large humanoid stood silently watching, its head titled curiously. "Ay ay they must really zigg their minds with it that is why they never speak ay!" "Ay Tura I wonder what it does to their mediations...the Psionics they can do...if we learned their psionic meditations… why I know we could explore the Salvi systems. While they are zigged!" Tura and Seti laughed, their divis sliding along their neck and shoulders.

Suddenly Seti's tentacles twitched, and then straightened, as the female Opian grew quiet, her large lidless red eyes grew lighter in color to luminous white. Tura watched his young friend's expression become abstracted and dreamy. "Seti?" Her mouth opened slightly as if she was in some fleeting aroused state. "Seti? What..." Tura began but noticed Seti's bizarre expression of sudden confusion and bliss passed as quickly as it began. Tura's young friend was now staring silently at something behind him.

He slowly followed Seti's gaze to see the Salv curiously observing them. The two Opians and the taller Salv stood there for a moment in uncomfortable silence. The Salv, three meters taller, looked down at them with a dispassionate gaze. *"The Spheres?"* Seti said to the expressionless Salv. "Seti! Let the Salv alone; do not psi them now. Make a formal request at the Luminist Council where all our interfaces with them can be recorded and safely monitored." Seti glanced at her friend, then back at the Salv. "After all, they are always monitoring us...aren't you Salvi?" Seti looked into the Salv's large dark blue eyes. "Come, ay Seti?" Seti continued with Tura, and as they moved on the Salv remained...gazing at them.

VI.   THE LUMINIST COUNCIL

In the central Opian biodome, the Luminist Council had been in session for several Salvine hours. One hundred green and blue skinned Opian Lums stood in large circles around a giant rostrum. Thousands of seated Opians silently whispered among themselves. Seven Salvs sat silently behind the rostrum of Lums, their expressionless faces observing the Opians. Master Junal, young Seti's male parent, was speaking to the rest of the Lums. "The IDRIS-10 launch must go ahead as planned; our orbit will never come this close to the Lost Planet for several generations. It may be the only opportunity to study the Lost Planet and produce the clearest images of its surface." The seven Salv's large blue eyes turned to a purple tint, spiraling into red as Master Junal spoke.

Another Opian Lum, Master Niris, spoke: "Master Serjo would the Salvs permit such a launch if we tripled their Searine herb production, and allowed the Zaxxon probe limited passes of the Lost Planet?" Master Serjo was the sole elder Lum who alone could communicate telepathically with the Salvs and stabilize the effects of Salvic psi transference. Master Serjo stood thoughtfully before the Salvs.

In all his psionic communications with the Salvs, he had learned one thing; they thought highly and cared for the Opians. He knew they viewed Opian society as childish, dangerous, and in need of strict observance. He knew it pained the Salvs to transfer mental thoughts and extract Opian thoughts and brainwaves, and caused short-term neurological stress. One thing he could not understand was the Salv harsh refusal to allow any space satellite near the Lost Planet. All their scientific launches to take images of the Lost Planet's surface were denied by the Salvs.

Master Serjo slowly turned, facing the group of seven Salvs sitting soundlessly behind the rostrum. He walked over and genuflected before them. As he expected they did not acknowledge his presence at all. The Opian Lum took up a seated ritual posture before the Salvs and made the necessary ritual motions with his hands and divis tentacles. Serjo spoke audibly the ancient Salvine language he had learned as a Lum youngling - an astonishing feat for any Opian at such an age. The Luminist Council grew quiet with only a few soft whispers emerging from the Opian crowd. When Serjo finished he genuflected again and began mediation to allow the Salv psionic transference.

As quickly as Master Serjo ended his speech to the Salvs in their ancient language, the seven Salv's eyes began spiraling indigo, red, and back to blue again repeatedly. The Salv's skin color changed from dark crimson to lighter tones, purple and blue highlights in long curving patterns appeared, disappeared, and reappeared. Their divi tentacles slid along their bodies, wrapping and unwrapping also turned into patterns of alternating dark red and violet. The Opian crowd became transfixed and nervous.

Master Serjo's tentacles trembled and wrapped tightly around him. His eyes became luminous white, slowly changing. The Lum felt the initial wave of overwhelming physical stimulation as his whole body shuddered in surrendering to the Salv's grasp of incredible psionic power and bliss. Ten thousand light years of wisdom in lattices of liquid light crashed into his brainwaves. . The air was now a fluidic fog around Master Serjo. Consciousness became a mist of sensory immersion. The Opian's soul recoiled from reality, a noumena, ceasing to exist outside the linear and conceptual. Consciousness reflected an atomic void between outer space and Serjo's body.   Electric atoms in motion unveiled alien souls in constant stasis.

The Opians were all his children, he loved them so much, so childish, and barbaric compared to the wondrous species of the First Generation galaxies. The air around him became fluidic, he felt as if he were floating gently in Salvine pools of liquid oxygen. Consciousness became a mist of sensory deprivation; all his thoughts were flung and reflected by a vast stellar light in an atomic void between his bio-body and the Salvs, and all conceptual reality. A Salv was speaking to him, through him, and with him. Its name he knew was Zevyla.

Zevyla and Master Serjo spoke as one. Zevyla-Serjo's melodic voice rang out and echoed around the Luminist biodome chamber. *All these worlds, we harvest in peace. Except the Lost Planet. No probes may enter orbit, attempt no landings. "When the Trinity of the Watchers aligns in the skies of Salv, the Great Sleep will end…the floating Vajra Pyramids will upturn blackened as the cosmic night.*

Serjo's conscious-brainwaves pleaded the Zevyla-consciousness, *Please my friends, my masters; let us look upon the face of our eternal watcher. Let us see with our own eyes and not from artificial eyes of detestable machines.* The Zevyla-consciousness responded back gently, *It is too dangerous for Opians. One day when the great alignments are past, and the stars change the face of the great Spiral Galaxy, Opians will look down upon this world as its infant, and past home. Your future will be ours. In time. Attempt no orbits around the Lost Planet.*

Serjo-consciousness resigned, but he had to try to warn his beautiful masters. *I may not be able to stop the launch my precious masters. I will try…I will try to convince them. The new ones are more curious than ever I have known them.* The Serjo-Zevyla psionic transference was discontinued by the Salv as quickly as it had begun. Serjo slowly sank his posture as other Lums rushed to his aid. What amazed him was something he felt, for a split second, before the psionic mindshift ended with Zevyla. He felt a trace of profound sadness from the Salvs. What truly frightened him more than anything in his own life...was that he felt what he swore by the Lost Planet was a trace of fear from the Salvs.

VII. SETI'S TOOLA

It was never dark because of the Lost Planet on Salv. Then, Salv was never completely in solar light. The reflective light from Salv's Febula Rings rarely penetrated the giant lost intruder, hanging over the horizon like an eternal caretaker. Troillyps screeched loudly, gliding over the glowing green inland seas of Salv. An amphibian two-legged Tetrog two meters in height hobbled along the seashore, nose sniffing and snuffling for a meal.

A floating Zoyzee Jellyfish hovered patiently over the unsuspecting Tetrog and sucked it noisily into its inner foamy entrails. The Tetrog wiggled its legs as the Zoyzee inhaled one final time and began digesting the creature. Myriads of sentient Phylo plants of iridescent colors vibrated and twisted, chuckling and howling. Mists floated around the landscape, emitted by the living Phylo plants as they heckled and chirped at each other. All was iridescent and alive beneath the indigo Salv sky.

Inside a biodome belonging to Seti's toola, eight Opian Lums sat in meditation. Divis were winding slowly along their heads and lean shoulders. Seti contemplated her strange encounter with the Salv earlier in the day. The sensations left her faint, shuddering. She felt as if the blood and nerves in her entire body were tingling with euphoria. Seti felt blissful and alive, special awareness and time were in a long spiral of dissolving with her body. The Opian Lums eyes turned luminous white, then jade.

Seti's household concluded their sacred rite of meditation and prayer to the Lost Planet. Her father, Master Junal was the first to rise and speak to the others. "Seti was mindshifted by a Salv today. Though she claims she is unharmed, I wish at least one or two of you to escort her outside at all times." "Father, I was with Tura! We did not see the Salv watching us." Seti protested. Her toola-siblings, Teela and Kwai, would not hear any of her attempts to placate their toola-father. Father Junal was an old and cynical Lum; he knew what the greater good was for all Lums, particularly his own toola. "Father, Teela and I will accompany Seti to her zooda." Kwai said. A zooda was a learning biodome for Opian youth and maturing Opians.

"I do not need anyone to accompany me to zooda father! The Salv did not harm me." Seti complained. "And the next time you encounter a Salv?" Junal pressed his daughter. He did not trust Salvs, their mindshifts bled to much neural energy from Opians, especially Lums. Were they consuming Opian vital-force? What did they want with his daughter? Junal was greatly disturbed over the encounter. Such a violation should not go unanswered. This should be reported to the Luminist Council. Junal knew the Luminist Council had pressing matters, but he would bring up the issue for discussion. For now, he would ensure his daughter's safety.

"Seti I forbid you to contact any Salv or go near their biodomes." Seti's divis coiled at her father's demand. "Why not assign me an Ultra from the Opian army to walk me to zooda father?" Seti teased. "Then we can invade the Floating Monolith Pyramids and conquer the Lost Planet!" Her mother and other siblings laughed. "Enough Seti. It is time for toolanet." Junal assigned his household their labors to ensure continued health of the biodome. Then they would assist other toolas in their tribe by place on their heads visor-like devices worn just above the eyes that allowed them to project images of themselves into other biodomes of the recipient wearing the same device, called a *visi.*

"We must seed more Searine plants before the next cycle. Master Serjo has said the Salvs are asking for twice the number by next conjunction." Junal announced to his mate and Kwai, his oldest offspring. "More?" Kwai said incredulously. "Salvis already increased production last conjunction! Why demand more harvest, are they using it to zigg out of the galaxy?" he said. "They are already dozens of tribes reporting severe shortages for their own toolas. Many toolas cannot sustain the phylic count in their own biodomes, much less provide for the Salvs." Seti's mother said. "If it were not for the Salvs, our healers would not have phylos, or any infos to use." Seti chimed up, her divis twisting around her arms.

Junal knew his wife was correct. Severe shortages of Searine were being addressed in nearly every session of the Luminist Council. Searine was the backbone of Opian enterprise. Salvs used Searine to draw in with their much longer divis, using it to cleanse their bodies and damaged cells.

Searine also enhanced the development of their psionic abilities by linking their brainwaves to the resounding vital-force patterns of all living creatures and plant life on their planet. The aromatic plant was vaporized by the Salvs who exhaled them and inhaled from with their divis.

"The Council is also debating a joint satellite launch and surface probe landing on the Lost Planet." Junal announced and recounted the activities and debates of the Luminist Council earlier that day. "They won't allow it as usual father. What happens when the proposal is denied? Will the Scientific Assembly try to debate the Salvs?" Kwai asked. Junal knew such a debate would be fruitless. Salvs did not even favor orbital satellites around the Lost Planet save for rare occasion. Even so, the Luminist Council was suspicious that the Salvs had disabled many satellites that were launched in orbit around the mysterious world.

"It would prove useless for the Assembly to bring the proposal to debate with the Salvs. They would never allow a surface landing." Junal said. "Furthermore, the discussion was especially intense. Master Serjo appeared to suffer some unknown reaction or affect from his mindshift. He collapsed." Kwai and the rest of the household was surprised at their father's further narration of how the Salvs obstinately denied and refused further discussion of landing a surface probe on the Lost Planet. Junal wondered aloud how the Salvs would react if a surface probe landed on the Lost Planet. His divis twitched anxiously.

"Though the Salvs denied scientific proposal for a surface landing, surely father they will permit an orbital satellite?" Kwai said. "My precious toola, there are secret discussions in the Luminist Council and Scientific Assembly to secretly deploy a probe to land on the Lost Planet undetected. Speak to this of no one." Junal said quietly. "Father, the Salvs would certainly detect any surface landing on the Lost Planet. If this deception is already under consideration, the Salvs know of it." Seti said.

Master Junal knew his firstborn was right. What his young daughter did not know was that using the latest psi-technology, and new insights into Phylo-psionic meditations, the Lums believed the Salvs could not detect their intentions.

"We have the right to explore our planet, and the right to harvest our precincts as we will. We are not the playthings of Salvs!" Kwai exclaimed to the household, his divis coiling wildly. "They are an elite society Kwai. If there are other extrasalvian beings out there that can warp across stars then they too would be advanced beyond our wisdom." Junal tried to reason with his incensed Kwai. He knew his children were right and feared where the growing anti-Salv feelings would take his fellow Opians and Lums. Junal and the other Masters knew of the growing anti-Salv groups that were planning mass protests. He even heard unsettling rumors that several of these groups planned to disrupt Salv meditations and march to the Floating Pyramid Monoliths. Junal's divis twitched at the thought.

VIII.   SALV CONCUPISCENT MEDITATION

Vaporous glowing red and white mists emitted from a Salv biodome, cascading into the indigo skies above. Two beings knelt in deep meditation, their *divi* tentacles slid along their bodies. The two Salvs, Zsiji and Zilah, sat with interfaces their skin tones changing from indigo to iridescent violet to ebony and then to a deep crimson. An Opialyte Phylo plant whistled quietly in the corner of Zsiji and Zilah's artificial biodome.

Telepathy was the form of communication between the twins, the also communicated through bodily gesture, and aurally. Their voices were melodic and hypnotic, the most pleasurable to listen of all species in the First Generation Galaxies. Clairvoyance and psychic abilities were common and highly developed among the advanced species of the First Generation Galaxies. Species of the Second and Third Generations of galaxies did not achieve as higher levels of consciousness.

Zsiji and Sapia began the initial rites of Convergence last season. The two beings first encountered each other exploring the ruins of Zsaalya the Archon, not far from the Inverted Pyramid Monoliths. Maturing together had been the adventure of their generation for Zsiji and Sapia. They were on the first expedition to establish contact with the El'Esirians of the Pleiades star cluster millions of light years away. It was natural and fated the two star-crossed adventurers conjoin their consciousness in the living lattices of light that wove the fabric of space and time together.

Salv emotions and concupiscence transcended evolutionary impulses found in every species outside the First Generation galaxies. The melding was mystical, permutations during the Rite changed the evolutionary blueprints of the two mating Beings, cellular structure melded and morphed in erotic convergence. Zsiji and Sapia knew they were destined for their joint adventures to expand outside the old Salvine-Vinithii fellowships into the darkest unexplored waylays of the cosmos. When they chanted the first Solliliquoy together, their parents' lifespan expired. Salvs believed after the death of their lifespan, the body must be ceremonially burned and the Great Canticle chanted threefold, as the soul became a lattice of light, leaving through the divis. The body of light, the Salvs believed, became NOORI, the Prime Reality.

The ethereal wonder between Zsiji and Sapia began with traditional chants. Sung aurally, body gesturing and harmonic movement of their divis accompanied their mystical chants. The two psimate's divis danced and undulated ritually before the first generation. Three generations of erotic convergence occurred, periods in the concupiscence that conjoined consciousness, and permutated cellular DNA. The chanting lasted several alignments. Zsiji and Sapia stared deep into each other's golden eyes, in elegant synchronicity of telepathic consciousness.

The first generation of the sacred rite began. It would last the equivalent of one Terran orbit around its star. The entire three generations of the ritual would last three full conjunctions, or the equivalent of roughly ten Terran orbits around the sun. Living Phylo and Opialyte plants around and inside Zsiji and Sapia's biodome chortled and shuttered as the first generation between the two psimates began. Consciousness melded as the two beings shared minds and sensations. The need to meld physically with one another had been implanted in their DNA. Salvs were incapable of biological procreation. Their genome had been irrevocably damaged during the last Great Golam war with the use of biogenic weapons.

Sapia and Zsiji's divi tentacles undulated and writhed, coiling and twisting into the other erotically. Their skin changed rhythmically from deep red and indigo to light red, violet, and then completely turning to indigo again. Skin tone flashed and shimmered. Patterned spots on their divis and bodies also shifted and became bio-luminescent. Vaporous mists emitted from their undulating *divi* tentacles, cascading high above their Idrisi, or continent, into the planets lower atmosphere giving it a luminous indigo glow. The vaporous mists encapsulated Zsiji and Sapia's biodome in a nebulous indigo brilliance.

After several seasons of the undulating divis and dance of luminous light, Zsiji and Sapia touched their faces gently to one another. Euphoric desire broke out of their DNA flooding into every drop of blood, into every cell. Salvs transcended basic evolutionary emotions often found in many species of Second and Third Generation galaxies. Concupiscence emanated only during their sacred mating rituals. Zsiji and Sapia slid their faces along each other for several more seasons, or Salvic months before the first kiss. Vapor fumed from their writhing divis as they embraced and twisted their bodies erotically.

Their kiss moved deep into one another, uncovering their souls, lingering at a crossroads between thousands of light years of desire and a moment of bliss. The two twisting beings kept the kiss uncovering their minds layer by layer until only subconscious desire existed between the two. Their erotic twisting embrace increased in momentum over the seasons. Sapia's face slid along Zsiji's skin and divis, captivated in bliss that would never be redone. Their exotic vapor made the dancing tones on their skins and divis bio-luminescent.

Sensations washed over the two beings, encasing them in a trance of euphoria that spanned millions of light years. Dozens of stars within one-hundred thousand light years went supernova. The Metusis B Cluster crashed into the Cornea Nebula, as the two Salvs entered trance after trance of latent bliss. The air became a fluidic glowing mist around them. Consciousness peeled away into a mist of sensation, recoiling from whirling reality around them. Outside the linear and conceptual, their Katras reflected an atomic void between outer space and their undulating bodies. Atoms in the deeps of space exploded into nebulas, destroying the stasis of stars and worlds. Zsiji and Sapia's kiss deepened.

The generation of the rite seemed like a cosmic dream to them. No species would ever duplicate the fantastic, wondrous nature of the Salv mating rite. Their erotic grinding and undulating came to a momentous pause as their divis now encircled the entirety of their bodies. Time and space in their conjoined consciousness slipped away. The momentous pause hurled their consciousness into a chrysalis of deep darkness as the second generation of the concupiscent rite began.

Zsiji and Sapia's skin tone and patterned dots along their body, which Salvs found stimulating at the site of, flashed in luminous indigo radiance. The two Salvs' bodies began to meld physically into one luminescent Being. Their consciousness expanded into the unfathomable deeps of space. Metamorphic sensuality melded the hybrid Zsiji-Sapia into one radiant indigo Salv. For the Zsiji-Sapia Being, time and spacial awareness dissolved. Their skin, minds, and body became one permutation. Their hybrid consciousness explored the dimensions outside time and space.

Entire empires and galactic fellowships became aware of the three concupiscent rites occurring on Salv, including Zsiji and Sapia's. Their Being entered into trance after trance, as stars millions of light years away became hidden in the blackness of the void, overcast by the Salv vital-force. Lost beings sought out the Salv consciousness from the darkness of outer space. Zsiji-Sapia gazed into the living universe as seasons passed, the final third generation of their sacred erotica began. Their evolved consciousness, advanced from tens of thousands of light years of spiritual technology, synchronized with the First Generation galaxies.

Molecular eruptions formed nebulas and stars. On Salv, the three concurrent mating rites, including Sapia and Zsiji's created a significant planetary quake that cost the lives of nearly sixty thousand Opians. The third generation of the rite began as the hybrid Zsiji-Sapia gradually manifested their individual consciousness. The entire process of the second generation of the rite reversed as the fluidic indigo mist encapsulating Zsiji-Sapia dissipated. The skin of Zsiji-Sapia again began to flash from complete indigo, to violent, and then back to their natural red with indigo patterns and shimmering spots.

The Zsiji-Sapia hybrid began to shudder, morphing and melding into sights that would astonish and terrify a Terran mind. A luminescent indigo radiance permeated into the atmosphere of Salv, signifying psionic and physiological orgasms as the third generations of the three concurrent rites came to telepathic pleasure. Sapia and Zsiji's individual bodies began to take shape, morphing with their shimmering colors of their skin tones. Light convergence created new patterns of spots along their divis and entire bodies, signifying orgasm and that the two Beings were now bonded for the duration of their lifespan.

Divis still twisting and sliding along each other's glowing bodies, Zsiji and Sapia kissed again, sliding their faces along each other. Sapia's blue lips caressed Zsiji's sliding divis erotically. Sapia's divis undulated uncontrollably as she reached mutual telepathic and physical orgasm with her mate. The two female Salvs sensually uncoiled their divis around each other, sliding them along their bodies letting them linger with erotic sensation. All sensations, all the atomic consciousness they shared in the fluidic mist, all dissipated into a deep silence. No space-consciousness, no radial thought, no emotion, nothing. Sapia and Zsiji were aware of each other as complete Beings.

Zilah and Zeb had also just completed their sacred mating concurrently with Sapia and Zsiji. The four Salvs had known each other their entire lifespans. Zsiji and Sapia were the nostalgia of consciousness in a past existence light years away. Salv births, which they called *"conjunctions,"* occurred at random. No Salv ever witnessed the conjunction of another Salv. Spheres of iridescent crimson carried a Salv fetus down from The Lost Planet. After several centuries, the Spheres began to be less and less as the Salv species dwindled significantly in number.

One day in Zeb and Zilah's, and, Sapia and Zsiji's early infant cycle, The Lost Planet hung pale blue and yellow over the entire horizon casting its peering gaze into Salv. The crimson Spheres stopped descending into the Salvic sky. The four Salv psimates knew their species was dwindling. Memories of their species were dreamlike, a fantastic dream in their lonely existence. Aural communication between the last of the Salvs was rare, their telepathic connection was unbreakable and could span light years of intergalactic travel.

No Salv vocal communication was heard since the Great Soliloquy of Zejiss'ajra at the Third Soliloquy of Convergence., seventeen thousand conjunctions (a series of Salv birth cycles measuring time) before the birth of the four psimates. In Sapia and Zsiji's biodome, the two sat in meditation, smiling at one another after their rite that lasted the equivalent of three Terran years and nine of their months orbiting. Sapia tilted her head and spoke audibly. *Zsiji.* Her psimates golden eyes flashed as her indigo mouth shot wide open in awe. Sapia smiled at her psimates response. Zsiji's melodic voice echoed around the chamber harmonically. *Sapia. Precious to me. You voiced my name.* Sapia's divis fluttered. The two beings have never heard the other's voice aurally. *Sapia. Your name comes from the word for curiosity in our ancient dialect. It is your wondrous curiosity that bonds me to you forever. The universe is like our playful phylo orchard. Our adventures will take us to beyond the sleeping universe in the night of time.* Sapia smiled and kissed Zsiji, embracing her. *Awakening is coming* she whispered.

In one of the regenerative biochambers in their dome, Zeb and Zilah's iridescent skin changed from deep crimson to indigo. Opialyte Phylo plants whistled all around the chamber now. The trance was broken. Zeb and Zilah's eyes went from spiraling indigo to a prismatic purple haze. Zilah sung harmonically in her melodic voice. All noises and echoes on Salv stopped except for Zilah's voice. *We must go to the Watcher.*

Zeb's golden shining eyes deepened in curious wonder. *Why did you use vocal communication?* She also spoke audibly. *There others...they are dying. We have felt very few conjunctions in our meditations since the two of us were younglings. Zeb.* Zilah had only spoken his name three times in her life. The first, during his conjunction, the second time was right before the Syntinnid invasion as all Salvs sensed through telepathic connection with the beings of the

First Generation galaxies that the insectoid Syntinnid were looking to enter the Salv system through their bioships. The third time Zilah spoke Zeb's name audibly was after the death of their parents several conjunctions earlier.

The First Ones report no other Salv transferences in their meditations for nearly one thousand conjunctions. The Nepetoids and El'Esirians have felt no transference. Zilah's melodic voice echoed all around them somberly. *When I made transferences to the crystallite spiders of the Verbenaceae galaxies, I felt no Salv minds connecting. I observed few other Salvs in their memory-waves* Zeb contemplated Zilah's report. *If we are dying, then we must speak to the Seven. They must know Zilah. Why have we not gone to the Watcher? If the Opians learn we can no longer procreate, they will use this knowledge to their violent inclinations.* Zeb and Zilah were curious about the state of their species. This was no cosmic astro-harvest to ponder. This was the fate of their race.

Salvs evolved past the need for emotion thousands of conjunctions ago. The Salv Council studied emotions in other species for hundreds of conjunctions before Zaailah with her meditations and unique esoteric knowledge from her storied transferences with species across the First Generation galaxies created the Rite of Salvis Psychotria. Salvis Psychotria lasted one generation (one Terran year). Zaailah developed with the assistance of her mate, the mysterious rite to purge the Salvs of lower emotions. Emotions in the Salv genome once led to a violent biowar causing near extinction of the Salvs during Zaailah's lifetime.

Zilah...we must ascertain the last memory-wave of contact with another Salv by any species. Zeb's euphonic voice resonated in the chamber. Zilah contemplated her psimate's words. *Zeb, a slow evanescence of our species can only mean something catastrophic has happened.* Zilah knew there was a drastic shift in the meditations and psionic transferences with her precious Salvs. She knew she must go to her mother, Zevyla who was soon to return from the Opian Luminist Council.

Zilah's elder parent, Zevyla listened telepathically to her daughter's report. She and the other six elder Salvs who led their species also sensed what Zilah and Zeb hypothesized about their species. Only a few seasons ago, her friends Zsiji and Sapia also made audience with the Seven, reporting the same discoveries as Zilah and Zeb. The Salvs had come to fear the worst. There were no more Salvs birthing for several dozen conjunctions. Other advances species like the Nepetoids, the crystalline Iconian spiders of the Verbenaceae galaxies, the El'Esirians, the ancient felines of Juul, or the Draags of Ygam had all communicated they experience few or no transferences with the Salvs for many conjunctions. Salvs knew the twilight of their race had come, and that they had to act soon to save themselves from extinction.

Zsiji and Sapia sat in mediation in their biodome. Sapia remembered their adventurous space expeditions together with other Salv travelers. Salvs traveled and quantum warped through the space continuum in their sentient bioships using the Great Conduits built over a billion years ago by the mysterious Artisans. During their other meditations, aboard one of their intergalactic sentient bioships, Sapia remembered psionic transferences with a race that just might be able to assist them in their evolutionary crucible.

IX. KWAI AND JUURI'S MINDSHIFT

Kwai and his mate Juuri were working on completing their toolanet labors in their biodome. Their parents and siblings were out socially visiting other toolas. Tura was escorting Seti, Kwai's sibling, to her zooda, an Opian learning center. It had been four generations, four years on Salv for the Opians since the concurrent conjugal rites of the Salvs Zsiji and Sapia, also Zeb and Zilah. Kwai's and Seti's toola had no further encounters with the Salvs since Seti's encounter generations ago.

Still, her father demanded an escort for her, which Seti frequently avoided. During the three concurrent Salv mating rites that included Zeb and Zilah, Zsiji and Sapia, a significant planetary quake occurred, costing the lives of over fifty-thousand Opians. It was a tragic effect of Salvic concupiscent rites that rarely occurred. Opian tribes grew infuriated at the quake; the Luminist Council had ascertained the cause originated from the intense psionic and vaporous emissions during the Salv mating rites. When this was made public in the last annual session of the Luminist Council, Opian Lums and common Opians alike became outraged and despondent.

Juuri was helping Kwai maintenance their toola's hydrator. "Juuri did you know that Tura and Seti are petitioning for entry into LUMSCIEX?" LUMSCIEX was the Luminist Scientific Exploration Division that governed all planetary and space scientific activity." "Those two spacers want to fly in rockets. Seti and Tura are so brave. It is dangerous; I do not think they should go. I will petition for entry, but not as a Rocketeer, Kwai." Kwai's divis slid around his shoulders thoughtfully. "They will be accepted next season, father told me. He is friends with Master Sedriis from the Scientific Assembly." The Opian Scientific Assembly was a part of the Luminist Council and functioned as the governing administration for LUMSCIEX.

"Do you think it is dangerous Kwai?" Juuri asked. "Ay for rocketeers yes Juuri. The IDRIS-3 space rocket malfunctioned in orbit nearly killing all the crew." Kwai knew council relations with the Salvs were deteriorating with the Lums and Salv. Opians were growing increasingly hostile towards their Salv cousins.

Even with the rising ill sentiment towards Salvs, the Opians still harvested double the amount of Searine requested by Salvs in the Luminist Council sessions. Salvs used the Searine in their vaporizers that sped up the process of their cellular regeneration, and also was a vaporizing mixture in their antigrav bioships; powered by their psionic vital-force and quantum drive.

Kwai tapped the communicator chip affixed to his long hand, and spoke with his siblings who initiated the nanolink. Seti was staying late at her zooda, an Opian higher learning centre. He and Juuri were to acquire nanopads from Master Niris' toola containing thousands of petabytes of data needed for the next Luminist Council session in the approaching cycle. Kwai and his siblings knew that this next Council session would be pivotal for Lums and Opians. He knew Lums would defer to ancient traditions and make a formal psionic request to the Salvs for an artificial probe landing on the Lost Planet, in addition to the launch of newer scientific satellites.

He knew the Scientific Assembly had approved last season the LUMSCIEX entreaty for an Opian rocketeer launch into orbit around Salv. It had been a few conjunctions since the last IDRIS-9 mission with a crew of four Lums. "One season Kwai, I foresee Seti and Tura on an IDRIS rocket mission. They will make all Opians proud!" Juuri said, as if sensing his thoughts. Kwai was pleased at the thought and let his younger sibling know it. "One cycle they will make us all proud, Juuri. One cycle soon." "And I will build the IDRIS rockets!" Juuri exclaimed. "Ay precious one, and one day I will sit on the Luminist Council alongside father. And we will drive the Salvs off and be rid of their ever-peering eyes." Kwai said, as his divis twitched and shuddered with excitement. Juuri's divis trembled apprehensively with Kwai's mention of the Salvs.

Juuri did not know what to think of the looming Salvs, ever-peering into their minds. They scared her, yet she was fascinated and had never encountered A Salv. She longed to communicate with one, but her father and mother forbade it. She would watch them in awe during the Luminist Council sessions. Seven Salv emissaries always sat in meditation.

Any address or communication with them was conducted by Master Serjo according to the ancient traditions. Every Opian who could walk or even used a magnechair for mobility attended the Luminist Council. Opian mothers even brought their infants to the rare spectacle. It was a chance for Opians and Lums to see the Salvs interacting with them, even if it was telepathically.

Lums taught their Opian compatriots to observe body language how their divis moved about languidly communicating with Lum Masters and their beloved Serjo throughout the conjunctions. Many Opian youth and younger adults adorned their garments with the Salvic Eye, a pictograph of a Salv's eye that often marked the exterior of a Salv's artificial biodomes. The Salvic Eye was also seen by daring Opians near the bottom of one of the Floating Monolith Pyramids. It became a source of Opians identification with Salvs and their mysterious culture.

The two Opian siblings left their dome and set out to Master Niris' biodome to acquire the nanopads. Juuri insisted they travel a longer route to Niris' dome, a route that would take them past the central Lum religious temple; where Salvs have been sighted near in the past. "Next season at transzooda I shall complete my studies in exo-cognizance. We will examine psionic technologies, Kwai." Juuri said. Kwai's divis were twitching nervously as he noticed a Salv biodome in the far distance to the West horizon. "Salv sorcery. Who knows what they pray to? I expect LUMSCIEX to accept my formal petition in a few cycles. Juuri, do you see that Salv biodome?" Juuri looked, widening her large red eyes to improve her eyesight.

"Kwai lets hasten I feel strange, my divis are all stinging." Kwai's large red eyes squinted in concern. "Are you alright Juuri?" "Ay, we should hasten." The two Opian Lums quickened their stride. As they approached the central Lum religious temple, they caught sight of a Salv a few meters behind the Temple. The Salv was planting Weeping Triphylloid flowers in the groves near the temple. The Weeping Triphylloids were rare and difficult to obtain on Salv. Fully blossomed, a Weeping Triphylloid reached up to fourteen meters high, its iridescent blue and white speckled petals grew up to three meters long, with long wisps of willowed hair on the petals that lit up with a bluish flame when approached.

Juuri saw the Salv first, immediately sensing its mind and life-force. Her divis slowly curled and twisted around her shoulders and head in unconscious reaction to the physical stimulation she felt in sensing the Salv's psionic energy and force. Kwai's divis curled quickly and tightly around his shoulders as he caught sight of the Salv. He stood there silently, transfixed in watching the Salv. The two Opians remained where they were, and dared not move unsure how to proceed. If they continued down the same thoroughfare, they would walk right by the Salv. Juuri could sense the Salv became aware their presence several nanocycles ago, feeling their minds before they even came into visual sighting. Yet she observed the Salv working gracefully tending to the Temple orchards, planting new Weeping Triphylloids. A strange whistling, sibilant and harmonic, started from the Salv as it finally acknowledged their presence and looked directly at them.

Juuri held onto Kwai's long thin arms. Opians and Lums were shorter than their Salv cousins yet still tall and slender, retaining slightly more muscular mass than Salvs. "We should just keep going, Kwai." Juuri whispered. The Salv's euphonic crooning continued. Juuri and Kwai moved cautiously along the road past the multi-spired temple. The Salv's crooning resonated around them, making their divis writhe. As they neared the male Salv, it began to do something unexpected, startling the two already nervous Opians. The Salv began to approach them.

Juuri's divis curled tightly around her shoulders, while Kwai's divis slid wildly around his gaunt shoulders and head. As they stopped in their tracks, the Salv walked up to them, tilting its head gazing at them with his large golden eyes wide open. Kwai and Juuri remained confounded as the Salv stood there a few meters from them staring inquisitively. Juuri felt the life-force of the gazing Salv cascade around her. She sensed as if fluidic warmth was enveloping her body. Though there was no physical change, Juuri perceived the air around her warm and vaporous.

Kwai saw the Juuri's large red eyes becoming increasingly distant, beginning to shine faintly. "We know about the Camarilla, Salv!" The Salvs nodded his head towards Kwai curiously, flashing his golden eyes. "We Lums know all about how you enslave us! One season soon we will have no need of your elitist hybrids!" Kwai rasped. Juuri looked at him and whispered, her eyes glowing red and white. "Kwai, no. You must no speak of the Camarilla. It is forbidden." "Cursed Salv. Why do you do this to us! Do you wish us in chains?" The Salvs large golden eyes flickered momentarily. "Kwai!" Juuri silently scolded, her mind beginning to meld into the sensations of the Salv's mind.

Zeb gazed at the two Opians before him. Life-force surged between minds as Juuri and Zeb's minds became conjoined. The Salv could feel the fear and other flood of emotions from the two tremulous Opians. He could feel Juuri's curious need to discover the scientific wonders that stood at the periphery of Opian civilization in the next few conjunctions. Juuri's unspoken love and adoration of Kwai's adventurous spirit submerged in the Salv's consciousness evolved over ten thousand conjunctions, spanning a million light years of philosophic knowledge, scientific advancement, and a liminal understanding of the cosmos.

Juuri felt the life-force of a luminous being thousands of years ahead in biological and philosophic evolution. Her body convulsed in physical stimulation, oversaturating her central nervous system. Hundreds of conjunctions of thoughts and conversations between the two Opians melded into Zeb's mind. The Salv telepathically scanned Juuri's cognitive history, reviewing the emotive and psionic indicators of hundreds of conjunctions of her conversations within the equivalent of a few Terran minutes. Juuri's divis twitched as her face contorted in physical stimulation. Kwai held her tightly and moved toward Zeb.

One recent subject of frequent conversation grabbed Zeb's psionic perception. The Salv became visibly disturbed at the revelation, and terminated the mindshift. Juuri nearly collapsed in Kwai's arms, murmuring incoherently. Zeb extracted from the telepathic meld Opians intended to go ahead with artificial and manned landings on the surface of the Lost Planet. He also felt the emotive surge of anger from Kwai and other Lums towards the Salvs, growing exponentially. Kwai stood a body's length in front of Zeb, flashing his large red eyes, slowly coiling and uncoiling his divis. "Remove your Camarilla from our minds Salv." Zeb gazed into the Opian Lum's flashing red eyes and responded.

We are all one consciousness experiencing life as One. There's no such thing as death, life is only a dream of the Great Sleeper, and we are the imagination of ourselves. Zeb replied telepathically. Kwai heard, and felt the force of Zeb's harmonic voice in his mind. Juuri felt the telepathic response aurally in her mind like Kwai. Zeb looked at his fellow Opians sadly. He already instantly reported the emotive and psionic inclinations of the Opian Lums he discerned from the mindshift to the Seven. Zeb knew the Seven must now partake in serious meditations on the Opians. There would assuredly be difficult meditations ahead. Kwai and Juuri watched the Salv walk away with the recognizable fluid glide in a Salv. They continued their embrace for a few spare moments, watching the towering Salv become a silhouette in the indigo sunlight.

X.   FORBIDDING THE IDRIS-11

The Opians and Lums at the Council were in an uproar over the increasing frequency of Salv mindshifts with Lums and common Opians. It had been three seasons since Juuri and Kwai's encounter with the Salv Zeb. Only last cycle did Kwai persuade Juuri to tell Kwai's father, Master Junal. The Council was even more distraught at the psionic messages conveyed through transference with Minister Serjo. There were increasing reports of long-lasting neurological and psychosomatic illness resulting from psionic transferences with Salvs.

Psionic transference was always initiated by Salvs and never by Opians. Salvs usually initiated the transference without warning to the Opian who received the transcendent expansion of consciousness. Lums and Opians alike reported telepathic mindshifts of philosophic and intellectual knowledge thousands of years ahead of Opian civilization. Many reported lingering visions long after a Salv ended the Psionic mindshifts. Juuri's psionic link with Zeb left her ill and sickened. She had developed lesions along her divis and eyes. Emotionally, Juuri began to deteriorate secluding herself from the toola, remaining for long periods of time alone in her biochambers without food.

Much to the concern of Kwai and her family, Juuri ceased her studies at the transzooda. She refused to discuss the matter, nor engage in any social activity, even with Kwai her friend since she was a youngling. Juurii had become ill with a terminal disease known to Opians as *rencis*. It was one of the three terminal diseases that remained untreatable save for painkillers and antibiotics to retard the spread of resulting internal infections. Rencis was genetic in Juuri's toola; her father Minister Jaanah's two brothers and her father's sister succumbed to the disease later in life. Diagnosis at Juuri's young age was extremely uncommon.

Juuri's father Master Jaanah attributed the diagnosis to her constant exposure to radiation while working at LUMSCIEX propulsion laboratories. The Opian Scientific Assembly refused a formal petition the Salvs for medical assistance with rencis and other diseases at the Luminist Council. The Assembly believed that reliance on Salv technology would make them indebted slaves to the Salvs. At this Luminist Council session, the Opian Masters decided they would state their intent to proceed with the planned IDRIS-10 spaceflight that would orbit the Lost Planet with a crew of four, and deploy a satellite probe that would attempt to land on the surface of the mysterious world.

The Scientific Assembly over the past season engaged in an impassioned debate whether they should bring a formal petition to the Salvs for medical assistance in the Rencis Pandemic. Master Ojiri, the Proctor of the Scientific Assembly was shouting, "Why stop with Rancis? Shall we have them cure Mnemositis as well? Why not put them on board our rockets with us? Invite them into our biochambers, have them lay with our mates?" Opians and Lums nodded and chattered loudly among the clamor in the Council biodome.

The Seven sat in silent meditation behind the Lum rostrum, oblivious and indifferent to the commotion directed at them. "The Assembly has voted. Although the Zaxxon probe generated no conclusive scientific data, the motion to launch IDRIS-10 has passed. We present it to the Council for final ratification." Master Ojiri said. "What of the Rencis Pandemic? If we do not petition the Seven for a cure, at the very least we must ask for their aid in producing a vaccine!" Master Lindra said above several Lums also trying to speak at the same time. "We will poll the

Assembly for a formal petition to the Seven to aid us in the assistance of developing a vaccine for the Rencis Pandemic. Master Lindra, your third daughter is afflicted with Rencis?" Master Ojiri inquired. "Yes. That is true. If a vaccine can save Opian lives, it is worth petitioning for….just this once." Master Lindra replied. "We will poll for a formal petition, so be it. However, I am troubled that the Salvs would be content to let our races die. They are so unwavering in their refusal to allow any landings or orbits around the Lost Planet, yet they remain indifferent to our wars, and our pandemics. Are we their lab-mites to observe and runt their abominable psionic and scientific tests on us?" Opians around the Council biodome nodded and murmured their agreement with Master Ojiri.

Juuri's parent, Master Jaanah, spoke up from the dais where the Lum Masters sat. "Perhaps it is we who behave like lab-mites to them." Jaanah said, gesturing toward the Seven. "My daughter Juuri lies ill, perhaps at the last cycles of her life. My daughter's mind is my mind, her heart and my heart are together even though she outgrows my lap. Perhaps if I understood the Salv who mindshifted her, this could have been avoided. What did it want? We will never know because we cower in fear. It is time we stand to the Salvs, face to face." Master Jaanah addressed the thousands of Opians, nodding and gesturing in agreement.

"Poll the Assembly Master Ojiri." Master Niris said. The Scientific Assembly polled their representatives, elected for life terms to serve the body responsible for the scientific, medical, and technological development of Opian society. Master Ojiri's polling took only a few arc-cycles. The polls revealed a narrow support for the Assembly to request formally the Luminist Council petition the Seven. "So bet it." Master Junal said. "The Council will formally Petition the Seven. The motions are as follows: launch and orbit of the Lost Planet on IDRIS-10 deploying the scientific probe into the atmosphere; allocation of one-third of Searine production from Salv Vils to the Lum Vils of Vashtri, Neroon, and Jobol; development of a Rencis vaccination to quell the pandemic; finally the manned launch of IDRIS-11 manned by a crew of five to attempt a landing on Lost Planet." The rest of the Luminist Masters all said "Aye so be it."

Master Serjo looked over at the Seven, meditating behind the rostrum. He had been mindshifting with the Seven the longest of any living Opian Lum. His fellow Lum councilors considered him one of the wisest to ever sit at the sacred Luminist Rostrum. Serjo could sense the psionic patterns of the Salvs as they meditated.   Serjo felt the ebbing and flowing of their vital life-force. He knew the Seven would not accept the formal Lum petitions. Almost acquiescingly, he turned to face the Seven. Master Serjo still held hope as he began his meditations, preparing himself for the ritual of addressing the Seven.

"Master Serjo." Serjo looked up from his ritual preliminaries and prayers. Master Junal spoke quietly. "Our daughters carry the future of our toolas to the stars. Speak for us in one voice. The Salvs must listen." Serjo nodded quietly. The Salvs were logical, their race based on logic and passion; transcending base emotions when the Opians were still crawling reptoids. He knew their logic transcended Opian philosophic traditions and elder tribal shamans who led religious rites concerning the Lost Planet.

Kwai was sitting with Tura in the amphitheater listening to the Lum Masters. "Even if the Seven reject the proposals Tura, you know Master Ojiri has instructed LUMSCIEX to proceed with IDRIS-10 and 11. I have decided to submit a formal entreaty for the 11 or 12 launches. Seti is also submitting her entreaty." Tura knew of the Councils plans to hold a secret session without the Seven if their petitions were rejected. "How do we know they did not create Rencis? The reason they forbid orbits around Lost Planet or landings is maybe they harbor some sort of horrible secret Kwai." Tura said as Master Serjo began his ritual. "Ay. Maybe they have other Opians enslaved on Lost Planet. Or other Salvs must live there, they are at war with or are imprisoned!" Kwai replied. The two Opians discussed their theories about Lost Planet and the Salvs quietly as Master Serjo turned toward the Seven.

Master Serjo knew the Seven envisaged Opians as dangerous children, an undeveloped species that required constant and strict observance. He knew from the mindshifts and psionic transference that the Salvs were a dying species. Somehow, for a reason and logic that was millions of light-years beyond his understanding, Lost Planet held the key to the Salvs survival. He could not understand why Opians could never set foot on the strange world. Serjo slowly turned, making the ritual circumambulations around the Seven.

The Salv elder matriarchs sat unmoving in a semicircle. Through their subconscious bioweb that connected them psychologically and psychically, the Seven could sense Serjo's graceful ritual dance unfolding in front of them. To any Opian or Lum, the Salvs appeared in deep meditation. Yet what an Opian or even racially and socially superior Opian Lum would not see was the deep deliberations between the Salv elders. They would address the Opian need for assistance with the Rencis Pandemic, provided strict diligence was given to groups planning widespread protests in Salv Vils. Vils by Salv standards were an expanded network of biodomes; each serving as dwellings, scientific, and spiritual centers for Salv psimates and their offspring. Opian Vils were larger population areas possessing both rural and urban attributes.

We must provide the vaccination and accelerate convalescence in those suffering from Rencis, primarily it is fatal to Lums and according to our predictive measures, could wipe out entire tribes within three cycles. Zilah, one of the Seven, voiced telepathically to the Seven's psychic bioweb. *Searine acts as a contagion to Lums, during their mating. Lums have modified the chemical structure of Searine to produce it as a neural stimulant. Its usage is known to their Scientific and political administrators yet the use of the stimulant is not addressed in any social structure. Exposure to it during mating created a mutation of their common Rundo virus that many Opians inoculate as younglings.* Zevyla, another elder voiced. The Seven knew they needed increased Searine production necessary for the phyline isotopes that allowed them to power their living bioships manned by crews of seven.

Their bioships were powered by rare elements the Salvs used to power their quantum space drives that were capable of traversing millions of light years across galaxies. The rare isotopes were found only on planet Salv. Searine was a rare element on Salv that could be atomically harnessed into miniscule crystalline liquid that clotted in the planets low gravitation field.

It would resemble a drop of water shattered into dozens of smaller drops retaining their original liquid state on a microscopic scale. Opians possessed the nanotechnology to vaporize Searine flower-crystals into isotopes that Salvs used as vapors and mists to both inhale during ritual meditations and concupiscent rites, and also in their quantum drives.

Zevyla knew the Salvs were dying, no live births had occurred for hundreds of conjunctions. The Seven's transferences with hundreds of species in the First Generation galaxies yielded no detection of a Salv being born on any planet. No Salv could remember witnessing any live birth. The Seven knew one cycle far in the history of Salvic civilization, an Opian rocketeer team would land on Lost Planet and uncover its cosmic wonders. Yet that time was not in any near future. *Until next cycle, we must retain current levels of Searine production. Then it is permissible for the Opians to reallocate the Searine to their proposed Vils.* Zenobia voiced as Zevyla and the other six elders synchronously voiced agreement in their connected consciousness.

Zenobia was the guiding matriarch of the Seven. She was younger than the oldest of the Seven who was called Zoroa. *Our chimerical meditations divulged several Opian tribes coalescing to create disturbance around our biodomes and the Floating Monoliths.* Zenobia voiced. The others were well aware of the increasing levels of aggression from Opians, and plots to organize and act on their prejudices. *"The time of the sleepers is coming. It will begin with the tear. Until then we must limit all connection with the Lums and especially Opians."* Zenobia continued, her thoughts and contemplations echoing across minds and space.

Precious ones, a few cycles ago, I mindshifted with a unique Opian Lum. Zsiji voiced. *I observed the Lum and her mate, her thoughts were fascinating. Her psionic frequencies and extrasensory perception is the highest observed in any Opian or Lum. The level of intellectual and philosophic brainwave activity is remarkable for any Opian.* The others were fascinated by this transference. *Were you capable of identifying the Opian Zsiji?* Zilah inquired. *This particular Opian Lum resembles the brainwave patterns of Lum Zeb established transference with a few cycles ago as well. Zeb identified her as the daughter of Master Jaanah. Unfortunately, she has become terminally ill*

52

resulting from the transference. Zsiji voiced her response to the bioweb Zilah's voice emanated within. *I hypothesize the Lum I made transference with was not the daughter of Master Jaanah. The Lum I joined with was the daughter of Master Junal. This Lum is training as a scientist for their LUMSCIEX.* The others were intrigued at this peculiar Lum.

Surely, space-rocketeering is beyond the intellectual and philosophic capacity of this highly advanced Lum? Zephyra, another of the elder matriarchs commented. *During my transference with her, I sensed a remarkable predilection of curiosity towards Salvs. The Lums cognitive process resembles early levels of advanced psionic development. Her intellectual and philosophic proclivities center on Salv culture.* Zsiji voiced.

This is exceptional for a Lum. I will observe her further and attempt transference. The others expressed approval at Zsiji's intention. *Perhaps studying her psionic abilities further will provide us insights into the Opians' emotional pathways. Since Salvis Psychotria, we have experienced little or no success in understanding the evolution of emotion in other species.* The others pondered Zsiji's discussion.

Salvs had purged the psychophysiological impulse since the Rite of Salvis Psychotria. No Salv experienced neurobiological tendencies of emotion to which human Terrans, and other developing species so often succumbed. Zsiji offered a unique hypothesis to the Seven. *There is a unique species called Oms, in guardianship by the Draags of Ygam. Their psychophysiological responses to behavioral stimuli, such as the intricate responses to mating are fascinating and unparalleled among many other developing species.* Zenobia was familiar with the Draags and had interacted with them on many occasions. *Yes, precious Zsiji, according to Draag scientists, the Oms had destroyed their own planet several conjunctions ago.* Zenobia voiced into the Salv hive mind.

The Om planet is uninhabitable. In their language, they referred to it as Terra. Zenobia continued. *What a precious name for a world and its race.* Zsiji voiced to the psionic hive. *We must establish transference with the Draags and learn more about their interaction with the Oms.* Zilah telepathized to the others. *Agreed precious Zilah. Transference with the Draags always has accelerated our understanding of isogamous procreation and conjugal ritual. As soon as bioships are ready for deep space orbit, we must establish transference with the Draags. Their procreative rites will assist us again in generating our procreative genome. With the Draags knowledge, our species can be saved.* Zenobia voiced.

The Seven harmonized their bioweb telepathic discussion. Plans were communicated to leading Salv engineers to prepare their massive bioships for deep space travel, allowing the Salvs uninterrupted and clear transference of their psionic minds and thoughts to species throughout the First Generation galaxies. The Seven's telepathic hive deliberations would go unnoticed to any observant Opian. To Opians in the Luminist Council amphitheater, the Seven remained in deep meditation while Master Serjo assumed a ritual genuflection before the Salvs and made the traditional ritual motions with his body and divis tentacles.

Serjo chanted euphonically the ancient Salvine language he had learned in his zooda as a Lum youngling, a much lauded accomplishment. The Luminist Council grew quiet with only a few soft murmurs emerging from the Opians in the amphitheater. When Serjo completed the traditional ritual, he genuflected again and began mediation to initiate the Salv psionic transference. The Salv hive psionic web was already prepared for telepathic deliberations.   The instant Master Serjo ended his speech to the Salvs in their ancient language, the seven Salv's eyes began to flash, spiraling indigo, red, and back to gold again rhythmically.

The Salv's skin flashed luminously from dark crimson to lighter tones, purple and blue highlights in long curving patterns appeared, disappeared, and reappeared. Their divi tentacles slid along their bodies, writhing and uncoiling, turning into patterns of alternating dark red and violet. Opians in the amphitheater became transfixed even though they have observed the dance of flashing colors on the Salvs on several occasions. For the Opians and Lums, this was the climax of all their interactions with the Salvs including Luminist Council sessions.

Master Serjo's divis convulsed with the rest of his body, writhing tightly around him. His eyes bean to glow white, flashing and slowly changing. The Lum felt the initial psychological wave of overwhelming physical stimulation as his whole body trembled in surrendering to the Salv's grasp of incredible psionic power and bliss. Light years of knowledge and power in lattices of liquid light crashed into his reptilian brain. Air turned to fluidic mist around Master Serjo as his consciousness melded into the telepathic hive of the Salvs, all his thoughts coalescing in a mist of telepathic immersion.

His mind attempted to project a disembodied voice, a noumena separate from the reality of his Katra. His conscious voice reflected an atomic void between his mind and the Salv telepathic hive. Atoms in motion unveiled alien souls in ethereal harmonics. It was Zenobia who's voice projected and represented the Seven's telepathic hive mind this time. *Precious Master Serjo. Peace be with your Katra.* She voiced. *And also with your Katra.* Serjo's thoughts echoed into the telepathic pool of mind. *We will foster generation of a vaccine remedy for the Rencis pestilence.* Zenobia's consciousness answered inside Serjo's mind. *The young Lum you name Juuri. Bring her to my biodome. We will heal her.* Tears flowed freely down Master Serjo's large red eyes as the Opians watched tensely in the amphitheater.

We know many of your tribes suffer in hunger from lack of Searine production and over laboring. This will be the last season of Searine production needed at this rate. We must compensate for interruptions in production from Opians who have refused to harvest, and dissented. We must increase crystallization of Searine by twenty-five percent. Next conjunction our bioships will partake of a deep space expedition. Then Lums may redistribute Searine to your Vils as needed. Zenobia voiced. Serjo knew this would cause much more dissention and clamor common Opians who bore the brunt of Searine crystallization and harvest.

Precious ones, a demand to increase Searine crystallization by twenty-five percent will cause much dissent and protest from my people. I cannot guarantee... Serjo struggled to voice telepathically, but Zenobia interrupted his straining consciousness. *Our species is in danger. We must use our resources in peace to survive.* "I will do my best to reason with the Council but patience wears thin as the Febula mists my friends." Serjo voiced, his connection growing weak. The Lum Master had been telepathically conjoined with the Seven far longer than usual. Opians and the Lum council members around him were growing increasingly nervous.

And...my precious friends...the launches ... ah ... I...the IDRIS missions....my friend...Junal....Seti... Serjo struggled with the overwhelming vital-force of the Salv psionic hive. *Seti. The one you name Seti.*

Zenobia and the Seven's vital-force fluctuated with their collective hive interest in Master Junal's child. *My precious....Lost Planet....ah....what are the spheres...aay...* Serjo's transference with the Seven broke as his body convulsed he could still feel the hive echoing its resounding harmonic voice, nearly shattering his mind. The pressure on his brain became physically unbearable as Master Serjo collapsed.

Lum healers and council members ran to him at once. Opians in the audience began to gasp and murmur loudly as many stood up attempting a better view among the clamor. Seti rose and rushed quickly to her father who was kneeling aside Serjo's body becoming increasingly pale green. Seti knew her father and Master Serjo had been close friends since their early youth. Seti put a hand on her father's shoulder. Sensing a tangible wave of fluidic energy cascade around her, she looked at the Seven. Their meditation had ceased and they were looking directly at her.

Seti felt the incredible sensual physical stimulation encase her entire body. She trembled slightly at the sensual pleasure, as the air around her became vaporous and fluidic with pure energy. Seti's divis writhed in euphoric pleasure. Her eyes flashed white and red luminously, surrendering to lattices of light and fluidic vital-force of the Salv hive. Her reptilian mind cascaded into psionic power and bliss, as the telepathic immersion into the Salv bioweb hive began. Seti projected a disembodied voice separate from the noumena of her Katra. Her conscious voice echoed into the atomic void between her mind and the Salv telepathic bioweb.

The mindshift allowed her to see the crucible the Salvs approached if action was not taken soon the Salv species would become extinct. She saw her beloved indigo homeworld descend into war and violence, she saw fantastic and wondrous species across the galaxies that had all interacted and exchanged technology and culture in a confederacy of species that spanned thousands of galaxies. She saw how the Salvs harvested the cosmos, creating nebulas, collapsing and expanding quasars and pulsars with their tremendous psionic abilities and their mysterious vapor.

Seti's mind shifted millions of light years away from her home, across extraordinary worlds; over a cosmic vista of supernovas, moons, empires, titanic space whales, sentient gaseous creatures, sun-sized serpentine beings that could devour entire suns, incredible crystalline spider cetaceans whose philosophy and technology spanned an empire of ten galaxies, she witnessed the horrors of the insectoid Syntinnid across hundreds of galaxies, she saw the fall of the great Palashaad Empire, the birth of large lizard like creatures on a blue world orbiting around a yellow star. Seti's mind shattered across millions of light years and coalesced back into her own consciousness.

I will dream with you. Her disembodied voice resounded into the Salv bioweb of consciousness. Zenobia and the hive voiced in response. *We will dream together when the time is come. Attempt no orbits around Lost Planet. Attempt no landings there. Peace be with you precious Seti-sii.* The Seven ended the psionic mindshift as instantaneously as it began. Seti knelt on the ground, her parent, Master Junal, was speaking loudly with his divis twitching frantically. "And also with you my precious friends." Seti spoke aloud.

XI.   THE TIME OF THE TEAR

Juuri lay nearly catatonic in her biochamber. It had been several cycles since Juuri and Kwai's incident with the Salv Zeb. Some of the most well-known and proficient Lum homeopaths had attempted to remedy Juuri's state following her mindshift with the Salv, Zeb. All their attempts to alleviate her condition failed. Master Junal's toola visited Juuri and remained at her side constantly for many cycles. News of the spectacle at the Luminist Council several cycles (Terran days) ago including Master Serjo's collapse, and Seti's psi-transference quickly spread to other Opians who did not attend the Council session.

Seti knew the Rencis disease threatened to overtake her childhood companion. Compounded with the psychophysiological effects of the mindshift with Zeb, her nervous and immune system were deteriorating. Prayers to the Lost Planet were made for arc-cycles (Terran hours) in many toolas that had known Master Jaanah and his toola for many generations. Her friend and toola-zan (of the same tribe yet not biologically related, similar to Terran 'godfathers, godmothers' or surrogate parents) Master Jaanah, looked at her father grimly. "I do not know what to do Junal-zan. We have tried everything conceivable." Master Junal was thoughtful. Perhaps they had not tried the unthinkable.

"Jaanah-zan. Perhaps we have not conceived of every alleviation." Master Jaanah looked up curiously at Junal, while Kwai and Tura administered a daily injection of antibiotics to prevent infections from Rencis sores forming around her divis. Seti sat quietly a few meters away from the others. "We all know the counsel was made by the Seven." Junal said. "No!" Tura cried aloud. "The Salvis have done enough, don't you think?" He cried angrily. Kwai's divis twitched in angry agreement. "Why not invite their entire Camarilla? How do we know what they would do to her? Heal her perhaps, make her a psi-slave?" "No…no the Salv overture is sincere. What choice do we have?" Master Junal interjected. "Our best medical efforts have not succeeded in effecting any change in her condition Kwai." Tura and Kwai continued to show their resentment of the Salvs by coiling and twitching their divis.

"Father, the Salvs know what they did. They know of her condition, they know the chemical composition of Rencis, Qlippoxis, even Hexis. Why do they let the tribes of Kataan and Baali constantly make war with one another?" Kwai said as Junal's divis slid around his shoulders despondently. "We must not conjecture Kwai. It is the way of the stars we share our home with the Salvs. Perhaps they protect us from the horrors of outer space." "Or withhold knowledge that could end the tribal wars, repair biodomes that are falling apart, help toolas that have no harvest and struggle with the Pestilence." Tura replied. "Ay. We are their lab-mites. Their playthings." Kwai added. "The Salvic Eye, it represents the Camarilla. We saw it before the mindshift with Juuri." Tura said.

The Camarilla was the Opian and Lums pejorative for Salv society and the Seven. Salvs knew of the term meant to be offensive and insidious in the Opian language. Camarilla was the actual name derived from the ancient Salvine language the Salvs named their interspecies fellowship that spanned millions of light years across twelve First Generation galaxies. The Salv-Vinithii Camarilla was named in thousands of languages. The Draags of Ygam called Camarilla, The Katran.

"Junal-zan, even if I could accept the Salv overture and save Juuri, how would we make contact?

Master Serjo remains in a coma." Jaanah said. With Master Serjo lying in a coma from the psychophysiological effects of the mindshift, no Opian Lum was capable of prolonged telepathic contact with the Seven. "Master Seleyis is undergoing the psionic training to replace Master Serjo's emissary. He is the eldest, though training will take at least two conjunctions." Junal replied. "The Council has suggested you and I initiate into the training as well." Jaanah said. Without the rituals and psi-initiation we cannot retain Luminist contact with the Salvs." He continued. Junal's divis slid nervously. He knew Jaanah was right to agonize.

   "My mind is linked to the Seven." Seti said quietly enough for the others to hear. Her father and compatriots turned towards her in surprise. "Linked ay? Are you going on their bioships too? To fight the scary Bundhashoons? " Kwai mocked. Bundhashoons were fierce imaginary carnivorous creatures resembling an Opian with large amounts of fur. Opian mothers told their children if they did not finish their meals and be good little younglings, the Bundhashoons would come and take them away. Tura's divis twitched in ridicule at his sibling's suggestion. "Where have you been putting your divis Seti-sii?" Tura and Kwai laughed and hissed aloud. Seti ignored their contempt.

   "We will let Juuri die? Without even trying?" Seti asked her father. "We don't know what Serjo meant before he collapsed. Were their overtures sincere? Should we accept their counsel?" Junal asked. "Refuse and let Juuri die? What if I lay there father? Would you ask the Salvs to save me? Would you try father?" "Of course precious-sii." Junal said softly. "Even if I agree to this counsel, how by the stars would we communicate with the Seven…or any Salv to help us?" Jaanah wept.   Seti and the others were quiet. Kwai spoke up "Why not go knock on one of their biodomes? Invite them for a toola-meal?" Tura hissed and laughed at Kwai's further mocking. "Enough." Junal scolded his maturing offspring. "No father. They are right." Seti said rising up and leaving her toola's biodome.

Master Junal, Jaanah, and the others sat in quiet disbelief. "She is quite the Lumi." Jaanah smiled sadly at his old friend. "Ay." Junal replied softly, now worried over his daughter's intentions. "Do you really think she will go knock on a Salv's biodome chamber?" Tura whispered to Kwai, who twisted his divis apologetically. Junal scowled at his children. Jaanah continued to stroke his unconscious daughter's head gently in his gaunt green hands.

Seti left her toola's biodome and set out for Master Seleyis' biodome. The Lum was an elder on the Council, tall for even an Opian whose telepathic talents were matched only by Master Serjo. Seleyis telepathically sensed Seti's arrival and stood at the entrance to his biodome. He was one of the few elder Lums to live alone without taking up a traditional Opian toola. Seti approached and bowed to the elder Lum as a traditional display of respect.

"You knew I was coming. You know what I must speak of Master-zan?" Seti said as they sat together in the main chamber. Seleyis drank a fruit concoction with Seti as they spoke aloud, echoing their thoughts telepathically. "You have questions about the spectacle during the last Council session." Master Seleyis said. "The Seven and I shared transference. They spoke to me in my thoughts, in my mind Master Seleyis." "The overtures from the Seven were genuine. We should accept them. The vital technological and philosophic knowledge they offer could save millions of Opians." Master Seleyis said. Seti replied in her thoughts, conjoining her mind with Master Seleyis. *"It will save Juuri. "* Her voice echoed into his mind telepathically.

The Council will accept the overtures. The Masters and I have reached agreement. All that remains is to call session, but we have no way of contacting the Seven. I have not initiated yet. There are no others. Master Seleyis voiced telepathically to Seti. His thoughts resonated in her mind. *I will mindshift with the Seven. "* Seti spoke into his mind. "Seti. The effects of Salv transference are not to be taken trivially.

The two of us together are cogent enough for a successful transference with the Seven. Seti knew the two of them could make contact with the Salvs, and endure the incredible psionic energies of their mind transferences. "The Seven already knows we intend to make contact. Salvs know the thoughts of Opians before thoughts become manifest." Seleyis said aloud aurally. "The Seven knows I will come." Since her mindshift at the last Council session, she could feel in the deep of her mind and spirit the Seven's constant vital-force from their powerful bioweb hive. She could still feel their thoughts echoing in her consciousness.

"Then it is settled Seti. We must somehow make contact with the Seven. We must go to their biodome. I know its location." Master Seleyis said. No Opian or Lum had ever attempted this. Not even old Serjo, he thought. Seti also knew of the location of the central biodome occupied by the Seven during times of ritual meditation and extraordinary psionic telekinesis that shaped and expanded quasars, stars, and nebulas across the cosmos. "We will mindshift here. Where it is safe. Away from the others." Seti's divis slid and coiled in approval at the older Seleyis' request.

Lum shamans who guided the Luminist Council with their visions could only teach the Luminist Ritual of the Herald Katra, used since the first Opian communications with the Salvs through formal initiation and religious consecration. Lum shamans were an exclusive society of twenty-two Opian Lums, each initiated by the rest when a member dies and a chosen Lum replaces him for the duration of his life. Lum Shamans, called *Telemesca* by common Opians, used visionary dreams, meditations, psionics, and long complicated elaborate chants that often took several arc-cycles, to counsel the decisions of the Luminist Council and Opian elders.

Master Seleyis had not initiated by the Telemesca thought he was learned in the proper rituals to herald transference with the Seven. For the next few cycles, Seleyis secretly taught Seti the rituals and Telemesca chants Master Serjo and emissaries before him used to address the Seven and herald a ritual mindshift that counseled Opian culture. Seleyis shared the intimate tradition with Seti, unknown to her toola and Master Junal. Several cycles passed as Seti and Seleyis began the long ornate ritual chanting and gesticulations, even though the Seven were not physically present as in Council sessions.

The two mindshifting Lums meditated for several arc-cycles. Each time they telepathically transfused their minds within the Salv neural bioweb. They could not maintain a stable conjunction in their consciousness with the hive. Seti felt as if there was an impenetrable fluidic vapor her and Seleyis' thought projections could not breach. They could feel the presence of the Salvs all around them on the planet, sensing their thoughts that concerned knowledge and vital philosophic confabs within the Camarilla.

Seti could sense the hive intelligence deliberating on matters millions of light years away with species that were merging spiritual inclination with machines; she could sense their role as mediators between two galactic empires preparing for massive interplanetary war ten 100,000 light years away in an elliptical galaxy. Seti and Seleyis sensed their vital exchange of a three million year old song about to be chanted by the ancient Jaanda spider-mammoths; a song that would prevent Jaanda extinction by regenerating a long-dormant genetic anomaly in their genome. Their meditations revealed the Salv attempts to neutralize the effects of the world-sized solar Serpents of the distant Andromeda galaxy that had accidentally consumed the Pleiades Cluster. Their minds could see the cosmic interventions at the hands of the Salv, in order to foster their inter-species Camarilla.

Seti and Master Seleyis' minds and their entire spirits felt suddenly and violently hurled into the chimerical realities of the Salv hive; their less-developed Opian minds spiraled into the infinite diversities and combinations of the Salvic bioweb. Their consciousness infused with the hive. Seven disembodied harmonious voices sang out to their melding consciousness as one. *Join with us. Come, precious ones.* Their physical bodies convulsed in sensual euphoria, as Seti's and Seleyis' divis undulated wildly. Their large red eyes flashed brilliant crimson and white, the patterns on their skin began to glow bright emerald and white.

The time of the Sleep is coming. We will heal your friend. All your pestilences shall be alleviated. This is our gift to the Opians. Come precious Seti, precious Seleyis. Katra darkens. Seleyis knew, and telepathically merged his knowledge of the ancient word with Seti's hive-mind. *Katra is an ancient Salvic word. It is the vital essence of the Salv spirit that seeks to die after the body can no longer retain cellular regeneration.* Seti and Seleyis ended their meditation, suddenly feeling a vibrating sensation all around their bodies. A luminescent crimson sphere began to form around each of their bodies. The two Lums felt their consciousness project into separate bodies of glowing emerald and white light within the crimson meditation spheres. Consciously awake, they saw their spirits form ethereal bodies within the meditation spheres. The spheres rose and hovered out of Seleyis' biodome, towards the Salvic Vils.

Seti and Master Seleyis remained in their physical bodies inside Seleyis' biodome. The crimson glowing meditation spheres containing their ethereal projections hovered over and down into Zsiji and Sapia's biodome. The Seven were seated; their hands and divis were all joined, linking each physically. The Seven sat, towering over the Lums by nearly two dozen meters. Deep red and indigo in skin tone, shimmering dusts of light glowed in fantastic patterns along the Salvs deep red and indigo skin. Their lidless large penetrating golden eyes spiraled and reflected the deep cosmos as transference with Seti and Master Seleyis occurred within the bioweb Hive.

In her parent's biochambers, Juuri lay unconscious near death. Her light green divis patterned with indigo had grown pale over the last several cycles. Master Jaanah sat in his toola biochamber tending to data slips containing news reports between Opian tribes. Tensions between tribe Kataan and Baali had increased the past few cycles over the latest attack on Kataan-occupied Vils, disputed by the Baali who shared close ethnic similarities with the Kataan. *Nothing has been resolved the past several conjunctions.* Jaanah thought. Now to make matters worse the Opian Kataans were openly calling the highly religious Baali co-conspirators since Baali have been known to assemble at the Floating Pyramids, and use the Salvic Eye pictograph in their religious rituals.

Opian Kataans were the second largest tribe. Their tribe had the most engineers who crystallized the

Searine into vapor used by the Salvs and Lums. *Maybe they should read the Uridani Scrolls again.* Jaanah thought, referring to ancient religious scrolls kept by the Telemesca, all Opians believed the scrolls were sacred, containing moral and social guidelines along with vital philosophic confabs between Salvs thousands of years ago. The Uridani Scrolls contained some of the only documented aural communications between Salvs.

Master Jaanah, peering over Council proposals about the Baali crisis, did not notice Juuri's eyes began glowing white, spiraling into red then flashing to white again. Juuri's Rencis lesions liquefied and melted away. Her natural complexion slowly returned as her entire body became illuminated in an emerald and white radiance.

Vapor emitted from Juuri's divis as Master Jaanah turned and looked at the physical transformations surrounding his child. Jaanah was in shocked. *The Salvs! This is Salv transference.* While the vapor from her divis filled the biochamber in a radiant mist, as quickly as Juuri's body became illuminated in emerald and white light, it faded as her eyes slowly flashed to their natural deep red. Juuri opened her eyes.

"Father? Father!" She tried to get out of the bed and stumbled into Jaanah's arms. "My precious sii...I thought we lost you." "Father...it was Seti. Seti is mindshifting with the Seven. Master Seleyis is with her." Juuri said weakly. "Rest child. Rest." Juuri fell back asleep, the deepest most peaceful sleep she could remember as she dreamt of stars and wonderful extrasalvine races long gone. Jaanah let her sleep. All across Opian Vils, toolas saw terminally ill parents and children completely recover. Within seven cycles, Opians were in an uproar as their pestilences, including the Rencis Pandemic were cured in the vapor emitting from the divis of their sick and dying.

Kwai and Tura rushed from the LUMSCIEX complex with their mother, to Master Jaanah's biodome where their father, Master Junal had summoned them. "What did the Salvs do? Kwai shouted. "Kwai…" Master Jaanah began but Kwai and Tura interrupted. "This is some kind of sorcery by the Camarilla. This is how they will control us. First they heal us but then they will come for the Searine." Tura's divis twitched wildly in agreement. "Next they deactivate the militias, and then our atom rockets." Tura said angrily. "The Telemesca prophesized this father." Kwai shouted. "Where is Seti?" Tura asked. *By the stars, she could be a psi-slave of the Camarilla.* He thought. The Lum homeopath Jaanah had summoned to examine Juuri spoke up.

"Master Jaanah. It is the same with all the others I have examined the past several cycles. Juuri shows no trace of Rencis." "Seti is with Master Seleyis Tura." Junal answered, looking at his friend's now mature child beginning to stir from the commotion between her adult siblings. "Patho," Jaanah addressed the homeopath healer by his formal Opian title, *Patho*. "My thanks to you and your toola. Your katra will be writing on the standing stones of Lost Planet." "This is quite extraordinary. Nothing like this has occurred in our history. I, like all Opians I assume, am anxious to see how the Council addresses the Salv healings."

"Seti is with Seleyis? Why father? " Tura asked angrily. "Regardless of what the Council does, we must prepare. We are seeing Salvs more and more now. The Baali tribe reports Salv sightings nearly every cycle now." "There is news that several tribes plan to gather at the Salv biodome thought to be the location where the Seven assemble." Kwai said. *Yes I read the news dataslips of several tribes calling for a mass gathering at the Salv biodome.* Jaanah thought. "Kwai. Tura. I forbid you to attend any gathering near any Salv biodomes." Master Junal spoke to his adult sons. "No father. The Salvs are aligning for something. The Telemesca warned us in their prophesies." Tura answered. He and his brother knew the Salvs were planning something ever since demand for Searine increased by a third of current levels.

Mindshifts were becoming more frequent. Tura thought. *Why were the Baali and others intent on gathering at Salv biodomes? Are they really going to halt their own distribution of Searine to the Council?* All Searine production was distributed to the Opian Lums, who administered Opian society. Opian Lums were an ethnic tribe that governed the rest of the tribes during Council sessions, including Kataans and Baali Opians. Kwai knew the Salvs could crystallize their Searine for their vapor and bioships, yet the covenant between Opians and Salvs dated back about a thousand conjunctions. *Moreover, where was Seti!* He wondered.

"We must return to LUMSCIEX in two cycles. By next alignment, our training will conclude father." Kwai said. "Tura-sii. Seti-sii. I want you to know the Salv transference saved Juuri's life." Master Jaanah spoke to his old Council companion's mature offspring. "Let the Council address this. This is the way it has been done for hundreds of conjunctions." Junal twitched his divis in agreement with his old friend. "In light of the events of the past few cycles, the Council will convene session without the Seven." *For the first time in one hundred conjunctions.* Junal thought.

"Council will not convene in the Lum Amphitheater. It will convene in the Temple of the Telemesca." Jaanah informed his sons. *And it will be like watching an Opian wrestling two Turogs from a Zoyzee.* He thought. The Council will convene at the end of the season. The next cycle, one cycle before Kwai and Tura were set to return to their training at LUMSCIEX, their father summoned them. Seti had not returned from Seleyis' biodome. Seleyis had communicated with the Lum Council asking his fellow Lums to grant him leave until the end of the season when the Council would convene in secret. Seleyis informed the Luminist Council that Seti and he had established psionic transference with the Seven. Later that cycle, he reported that Master Serjo had died from complications related to his mindshift during the last Lum Council.

Junal informed his sons of the news. "Seti remains at Master Seleyis' biodome. She is safe." Tura and Kwai's divis writhed angrily. "She is becoming a psi-slave to them father!" "Kwai. Tura. Master Serjo has released his katra to the Lost Planet." "May his katra live again in the light of Katran." Tura gave the traditional religious response to the news of an Opian Lum's death. Kwai's and Tura's divis twisted and uncoiled along with their father's in the traditional gesture.

"The Salvs took his katra. They ripped it from his body." Tura said after a long silence. "And they made Seti a psi-slave." "No Tura. Seti has joined her katra with the Seven. I felt her in the Salv hive. She communicates with them." Juuri said awakening from an entire cycle's sleep. "You awaken Juuri-sii. How can we ascertain fully the effects of the transference on you?" Kwai asked his childhood friend. "Granted, the mindshift cured the Rencis, and within cycles you made a full recovery according to the patho." Tura said. Juuri's divis slid along her shoulders apprehensively. "I was healed. How many others were saved?" She said. "Saved to be psi-slaves. And taken aboard their bioships as psi-slaves. By the stars I bet they feed from us in their bioships!" "Enough." Jaanah said. The funerary ritual for Serjo was to be held in the next three cycles.

Kwai and Tura would return after Master Serjo's Lum funerary ceremony. All on the Luminist Council would attend, including thousands of Opians. "We must see Seti." Kwai said as he and Tura left the biodome. They set out for Master Seleyis' biodome and arrived at the entrance several arc-cycles later. The indigo horizon on Salv was illuminated with glowing blue and green mists. Myriads of living Weeping Triphylloid and phylo plants of iridescent colors vibrated and twisted, chuckling and howling all around the Vil where Seleyis' biodome was located.

Vapors floated around the landscape, emitted by the living Weeping Triphylloid plants as they heckled and chirped at each other. Two Howling Zephyrids glided and swooped down on a stumbling Tetrog, letting out their distinguishable howls as they dove in for their evening dinner. The indigo night howled, chuckled, and sang.

As was customary for Opian Lums, Master Seleyis' door was open to his biodome. A traditional bowl of fruits was left out for passersby. Kwai and Tura announced their presence. Hearing no response, the two slowly entered the biodome, large by Lum standards. Kwai felt his skin tingling as his divis reacted to a sudden wave of sensual pleasure. Tura felt the same arousing sensations. The two could see the vaporous mists floating around inside. Tura and Kwai become very confused. Their minds were filling with thoughts and sensations that were not their own.

Their red eyes began to sting as their vision became difficult. Slowly with great effort, they stumbled, following the vapor's trail into Master Seleyis' inner study biochamber. The large spacious study chamber was dimly lit with candlelight. Tura and Kwai shouted in disbelief at the bizarre sight before them. Seti and Seleyis' sat in meditation, a red luminous meditation sphere formed above them. Their ethereal katra bodies projected and formed within the meditation spheres. Sitting on the other side of the shadowy study chamber were the Salvs Zsiji and Sapia.

The two Salvs were conjoined, their bodies morphing and melding into bizarre serpentine shapes. The fantastic site before Kwai and Tura caused them to yell in fright and stumble out of the biodome. "My head….my divis…" Tura groaned and hissed. "What by the stars was that? What did they do…what…" Kwai hissed. The two Lums ran back down an esplanade they thought was familiar and would take them to their toola biodome.

They were mistaken. The esplanade led the two down unfamiliar paths. They saw Weeping Triphylloids, living Zephytrope plants and dozens of other bizarre moving plants, opening and closing, growing and shrinking into various petals and stems. All sorts of harmonious chortling from the Phylos, twittering from the Zephytropes, and bellowing from large violet and spotted yellow plants the two had never seen, assailed their divi senses.

The two came to a huge biodome they thought resembled an ancient Lum temple, surrounded by orchards, and standing stones. Suddenly they heard a melodic sibilant voice echo within their minds. *"Do not be frightened. Seti is unharmed. Come, precious ones."* Kwai shouted out in distress as his and Tura's tentacles twitched wildly. Turning behind them, they saw a Salv standing, observing them with her head tilted in curiosity.

Tura grabbed his head in distress as Kwai moved forward toward the Salv. He pulled his *benta* shaft from his tunic and started toward the Salv. He pointed the shaft at the Salv. " What are you?" Kwai walked up to the Salv towering a few meters above him. A wave of sensual euphoria suddenly overwhelmed him as his body convulsed in pleasure, his divis sliding along the Salv female. The Salv crouched down and let her divis slowly entwine with Kwai's. Weeping Triphylloids, living Zephytrope plants and dozens of other bizarre swaying plants chortled and sung wildly.

Kwai's body shuddered in euphoria as he involuntarily moaned and hissed. Tura had crouched to his knees to prevent falling from falling over. When the pain subsided in his head, he grabbed his own benta shaft and swung it at the Salv female's divis. He hit the Salv with such force, she let out a high pitched shriek. The Salv pulled back and looked at Tura and Kwai in horror. Kwai had collapsed to the ground in pain.

"Let's flee, now Kwai!" Tura grabbed him as the two ran, stumbling back down the esplanade. Zenobia stood there in horror and dismay. Never had an Opian attacked a Salv. Zenobia felt an unfamiliar sting on her divis. Reaching up and touching it tenderly with her hands, she lowered her hand and saw it smeared with her own blood. Zenobia gazed back towards the fleeing Opians. A tear formed and slid down her eye.

"It has begun." The Seven voices harmonized in every Salv mind. Across the indigo jewel in the cosmos, Salvs lowered their heads, and knew.

XII. ORBITAL ECLIPSE

Tura and Kwai did not speak of their encounter with Zenobia. Tura now worked at LUMSCIEX with his sibling Kwai, as a biochemical engineer. Kwai successfully passed the physical and intellectual prerequisites for a rocketeer aboard the IDRIS-10 outer space mission. The rocket carried a Zaxxon-II satellite that would deploy around orbit of the Lost Planet. Salvs had approved the launch of the satellite during the last Council session and transference with Master Serjo. IDRIS-10 also carried a secret payload, the METRIS rover code-named "Catarina" by scientists at LUMSCIEX.

Scientists and Lums referred to "Catarina" as a space bioengineering laboratory attached to the Zaxxon-II satellite. The ruse was intended to fool the Seven. Kwai, the rocket pilot Jiro, and three other Lum rocketeers. Kwai's position on the mission was as a co-pilot, operating the internal controls of the space rocket. Kwai spoke only to Tura about their encounter several cycles ago. He had never felt such euphoria and physical pleasure before in his life, even during mating. The confrontation greatly disturbed him, more than anything the Salv's display of psionic vital-force light years beyond any Opian or Lum capability.

Juuri spoke with Kwai and Tura outside the LUMSCIEX bioscience chambers, where Kwai was checking his space suit, preparing for the mission. "Do you think Catarina will succeed?" "Of course, Juuri. Salvs do not know the real purpose of Catarina." "What do you think Catarina will find Kwai?" Juuri asked, sliding her divis thoughtfully along her shoulders. "The potential for scientific and cultural discoveries on Lost Planet are far beyond anything we could imagine Juuri." Kwai replied. *If the scientific and cultural possibilities of discovery are beyond our imagination, why do the Telemesca oppose any landing on the surface as sacrilege?* Kwai thought.

"We could discover the origins of Salv civilization." Juuri grew excited thinking about what mysteries they would potentially uncover on Lost Planet. "We could see if Lost Planet is where the Salvs came from. Alternatively, if they have slaves there. Opian slaves!" Kwai exclaimed. "Unlikely. The Salvs are peaceful and saved millions of Opians. Why would they keep slaves Kwai?" Juuri coiled her divis disapprovingly. "Benevolence and Goodwill do not necessarily mean one has benign intentions Juuri." Kwai replied. "Recall the last great Baali Empire, how they built the Coridian aqueducts, and the great transzooda academies of the Valtrex. They ended the reign of Kelva the Maulth. Yet, in fact the Baali Empire was the most feared and oppressive in history." Juuri knew Kwai was right. The Baali tribe did a great many seemingly benevolent acts, yet caused the bloodiest war in Opian history.

"The Salvs could have destroyed the Lost Planet long ago Juuri. The Stars only know what secrets they keep hidden away there." Jiro, the IDRIS-10 pilot entered and overheard Kwai and Juuri talking. "Juuri-sii, I am pleased you are well. You look as beautiful as a Weeping Zephyria" The patterns on Juuri's divis turned dark blue. "Thank you Jiro." Juuri chuckled. Kwai coiled his divis irritably at Jiro who pretended not to notice. "We suit up for preflight at 3370 arcs old friend." "I will be ready." Kwai replied. Jiro left the chambers, waving his divis at Juuri. "Farewell Jiro." She laughed quietly.

"Kwai do you think they will permit Seti on the IDRIS-11 mission?" "Juuri! We should not even discuss the mission. It is restricted." "But no, Master

Niris came to visit me and said the Council wants Seti onboard, due to her extensive interaction with the Salvs." *If that is true, then the Council knows more than they are letting on.* Kwai thought. *I must speak with father.* "I do not know Juuri." He said. "Our mission is critical. If Catarina fails, the Assembly will poll on whether we should even launch IDRIS-11." "Kwai. Something has been on your mind. Burdening you. I know you are troubled by what the Salvs did to me." "They saved your life. But there are serious sufferings greater than we know. Tura and I saw something horrible the other night."

"Tura and I visited Master Seleyis' biodome, and found two Salvs there. With Seleyis and Seti!" Juuri's eyes flashed at Kwai's story. "The Salvs were conducting some bizarre experiment. They were….changing….horribly." "Changing?" Juuri asked nervously. "They were changing…form and shape. And so were Seleyis and Seti….I cannot begin to describe how terrible it was." Kwai's divis were twitching hesitantly. *If only you could have seen the treacherous horror.* Kwai thought. *And what the Salv did to me.*

"Kwai what happened. What did you see?" "They changed Juuri. Their bodies changed, and….there was two of Seti and Seleyis. Their bodies were…replicated somehow…encased in a large red glowing sphere. I could not tell which body was real!" Juuri's eyes flashed in surprise. "They had two bodies? Like their katra? Where they incorporeal?" Juuri asked him. "I do not know. It was an unspeakable appalling sight." Juuri slid her divis around her shoulders and torso, trying to imagine the fantastic vision. "There is more. As we fled, we encountered another Salv. Tura confronted her, with his benta." Juuri lowered her head. *His katra only knows what he set forth with his actions.* Juuri thought. "The Salv….violated my mind…it felt euphoric…as if….I was mating." *Ay were you thinking of mating with the Salv or me?* Juuri thought.

The Salvs saved her life. Rencis certainly was in its final stages. Juuri had tried inhaling the vapor from the crystallized Searine used by the Salvs in their meditation rituals. *It brought me closer to understanding the Hive. I can feel thoughts and sensations of others in my own mind. I can feel how they feel.* Juuri wondered if millions of Opians saw their psionic abilities change once they were cured. *Or where they too scared to speak of it aloud?* "They can do whatever they want to us Juuri. The amount of power and control they have. They can snap our minds and shatter our katra if they wanted. We are already their slaves." Juuri knew Kwai was right. With such power, Opians and Lums have always been at the mercy of Salvs.

"Why would they remain on our planet if they can travel to other worlds?" Kwai wondered aloud. "They must have a purpose for continuing to live on our planet and watch over us." Juuri offered, but she could not escape Kwai's prejudiced logic. Why would the Salvs stay on the planet? Certainly, their quantum bioships could take them anywhere? "Conceivably they are protecting us from something or exploiting Opians for their own purposes which we are all unaware." Kwai said. "Whatever power source drives their bioships, it is far beyond any technological achievement Opians could hope for in a thousand conjunctions." "Ay but Kwai, why have no other beings come to our planet and made themselves known to us? Are Salvs preventing other beings from coming to us?" "It is possible Juuri. One thing I know is that the Camarilla are not what they appear to be. There is more to Salvs than we can fathom. And I feel their benignity is a façade." Juuri lowered her head. Kwai's logic again was sound. Why did the Salvs save her and millions of other Opians?

The next cycle Jiro, Kwai, and the rest of the IDRIS crew were putting on their protective launch suits shielding them from the IDRIS rocket's radioactive fuel, and the gamma vapors in the lower Salvic atmosphere. The whole process took several arc-cycles and soon the rocket crew boarded the IDRIS-10 rocket to synchronize and calibrate on board instruments for launch into orbit. The Lum Council Masters observed the launch on ion display units from the Council guest chambers.

The LUMSCIEX launch proctors completed the launch poll within their respective stations. Jiro, Kwai and the rest of the rocket crew sat inside the IDRIS-10 control capsule awaiting confirmation of launch. "IDRIS SCIEX Mission Proctor confirms launch is so." "SCIEX. IDRIS. Recognized. Launch is so. We will meet you on dataslip zed." "IDRIS. SCIEX. To the stars and into the void. Honor to you and honor us all, that we may learn more about ourselves." Jiro and Kwai nodded at one another. The last sentence was code that the Catarina probe was ready and operating. They would deploy the probe and direct it to land on Lost Planet, in order to uncover its mysteries.

Within an arc-cycle, the rocket was ready to launch, the seventh mission to have a live Opian crew. "IDRIS. SCIEX. Sequence hold release. Launch in Count-set 140 arcs...." "SCIEX. IDRIS. Recognized. 140 arcs...." Jiro instructed the crew to prepare for launch via his interlink communicator. Kwai monitored the ion regulators and plasma gauges. All seemed sufficient; there were no indication of problems. "70 arcs..." LUMSCIEX launch proctors continued the final stage of the launch countdown. "30 arcs...20 arcs...10 arcs..." The rockets engines whined and roared. A stream of blue and white plasma followed the rocket through planet Salv's upper atmosphere.

Seti sat in Master Seleyis' biodome observing the launch on Master Seleyis' ion display unit. Seleyis' observed the launch with her. "The Council is holding session in a few cycles. In the Temple of the Telemesca." Seleyis said, watching the launch intently on the ion display. "The Seven know of it. Zenobia said the Council and all Opians need sincere dialogue without Salvs present." Seti replied. Zenobia and the others believe I should go aboard IDRIS next season." "Will you go?   The Salvs trust you. You could be the first Opian ever to land on Lost Planet." *If the Seven allow it.* Seti thought, letting her thoughts telepathically resound throughout Seleyis' mind.

"I must report to SCIEX to complete launch training." *What will you confer with the Seven?* Seleyis voiced within her mind. *I will listen to them, and they to me Master.* Seleyis' divis slid sympathetically, feeling Seti's voice in his mind. *Something greatly burdens all Salvs. A deep disquiet, like sadness.* Seti voiced telepathically. *The Salvs keep their secrets. Some of their deepest knowledge of the universe we must never know. We are not ready. Yet they are keeping something from us. Something dangerous that could destroy Opians and Salvs. Part of that secret lies on Lost Planet.* Seleyis replied clairvoyantly. *And that is why I fear what we Opians may find there.* Seti kept her thoughts hidden.

Three cycles after the IDRIS rocket launch, the crew diligently entered in computer commands for robotic arms inside the rocket to deploy the Zaxxon-II satellite that would orbit Lost Planet and secretly deploy the METRIS planetary rover. "Inertial upper stage complete Principal." Jaali, a crew engineer informed Jiro, the mission leader. "Recognized." Jiro replied. "Artificial Manipulator Array stationed." A

Lum robotic engineers said over his communicator. Kwai calibrated the controls of the Robotic Assist Module that would deploy the Zaxxon-II probe and METRIS rover. The Lum rocketeer check and verified their position in geosynchronous orbit. "Principal Jiro, we are stationed 3.141 degrees zenith over Lost Planet. AM Array in position for deployment." Kwai announced to Jiro and the crew.

"Recognized. Commence deployment Kwai. 00314 nanos. Dataslip 3-Zed." Jiro instructed. Kwai began the sequence that slowly moved the rockets robotic arm in deploying the probe. Within a few arc-cycles, the slow diligent process was complete. The robotic array's artificial arms released the probe into outer space above Lost Planet. Kwai programmed in commands that fired the plasma thrusters on the probe, as it began descent into the atmosphere of Lost Planet.

"SCIEX. IDRIS. Zaxxon deployment is so. Orbit achieved. Mesospheric entry in one arc-cycle. Awaiting Catharsis command." Jiro radioed SCIEX control proctors on his ship transmission unit. "Catharsis Command" was their coded phrase from SCIEX to deploy the METRIS planetary rover, code-named 'Catarina,' and begin its descent to the surface. "IDRIS. SCIEX Proctor. Await confirmation of Catharsis Command." "SCIEX Proctor. IDRIS. Recognized." Jiro replied. He looked at his friend Kwai. Jiro could sense how anxious Kwai and the rest of the crew were about deploying Catarina and its descent onto Lost Planet's surface.

The mission proctors relayed the request to the head Proctor of LUMSCIEX, who transmitted Master Ojiri, the Council Proctor representing the Scientific Assembly. Ojiri conferred with his Council friends Master Lindra and Master Niris. "The Salvs know of our enterprise with Catarina. It is too late to withhold the command." Ojiri said to his fellow counsel.

"Perhaps they will not stop us." Master Lindra replied. Ojiri and Niris slid their divis around pensively. "We could hold Council in the Temple of the Telemesca first. And poll the Council whether to issue the command." Lindra said. "It is too late. The Zaxxon probe is already deployed in orbit." Lindra sustained any objections from his counsel. "We must confer with Master Seleyis." Niris said. Seleyis and his protégé Seti, Master Junal's child, had recent transference with the Salvs. They would know the Salvs intentions.

Master Ojiri transmitted to Seleyis on his communicator piece. "The proctors at SCIEX are wondering what to do with the METRIS rover Seti." Seti slid and coiled her divis contemplatively. "We have nothing to hide. Let them deploy." She said aloud sadly. "It is time we began to know ourselves and make mistakes." Seleyis writhed his divis in agreement. The Seven cannot be our keepers anymore. *We must find our own destinies among the stars.* She telepathically voiced to her old mentor. After some deliberation, Seleyis returned the data transmit to Master Ojiri. "Make the command so old friend Ojiri." He replied into his communicator. *May my Katra forgive us if I am wrong.* Seti thought, hiding her telepathy from Seleyis.

"IDRIS. SCIEX. Catharsis Command is so." The launch proctor communicated to Jiro several arc-cycles after his request for a decision whether or not to deploy the secret planetary rover. "SCIEX. IDRIS. Recognized. Catharsis is so." Jiro communicated back to Salv. "Deploy Catarina Kwai." Kwai entered in the command code to the Zaxxon-II probe what would deploy the METRIS rover. Within an arc-cycle, the METRIS planetary rover entered Lost Planet's atmosphere, beginning its descent to the surface. "Principal, Catarina entering mesosphere in 70 arcs."

Kwai informed Jiro. Suddenly, the rockets instruments began to go wild and sound alarms.

Crewmembers all spoke at once shouting out warnings to Jiro as they crouched over their stations. "Readings are off the scale, Jiro. All communication links are down!" Kwai shouted over the commotion. As the Catarina rover descended through Lost Planet's mesosphere, an iridescent red sphere discharged up from the Lost Planet. The glowing crimson orb blasted the METRIS planetary rover into oblivion. A second iridescent crimson orb discharged from the planet, shooting quickly through the atmosphere. "Principal..." A frantic crew engineer began. "I see it..." Jiro replied. The fiery red orb was headed straight for the Zaxxon-II satellite.

The IDRIS rocket began to lose orbit, as the ships communications came online and offline intermittently. The launch proctors on planet Salv received a final garbled message from the crew: "flashing spheres...SCIEX do you recognize?.... Catarina...like an eclipse..." The launch proctors looked at each other stunned. "We have to get them down." One of the launch Proctors said. Divis coiled in anger and red eyes flashed on Lums and Opians around the control panels. "This was the Salvs." One of the proctors said. "Another Camarilla plot." The communications Proctor said coiling his divis angrily.

Several cycles later Jiro and Kwai huddled around the rocket control console. The internal environment regulators and gravity had all lost power. The only operating consoles were the navigation and propulsion units. Jiro and Kwai were freezing, unused to the unregulated cold climate in the freezing rocket capsule. Salv's surface temperatures reached an average of 40 degrees Celsius. "The reserve capsule is manually programmed to return to Salv. We must divert all remaining power to the capsule." Jiro said weakly. "You are suffering from hypothermia old friend." Kwai said, shivering. His divis were already turning dark green, displaying his own symptoms of hypothermia. "We will use the rest of the crew meals, and their thermosuits." He said to Jiro. The rest of the crew had already died from the severe freeze and lack of breathable air in the capsule.

"Use the comms…cannot talk anymore." Jiro said shivering. The two Lums made their way into the reserve capsule, diverting all the rockets negligible power into the capsule in order to begin the auto-controlled orbital descent back to Salv. The reserve capsule plunged through the Salvic stratosphere, deploying its descent sheaths. The two capsule occupants were rocked around violently as the capsule dropped into Salv's small Red Febula Sea.

As the capsule floated in the sea, Kwai was barely conscious. He looked at Jiro who was bruised and frozen to death. "Ay Jiro-sii…" Kwai muttered and lost consciousness. The IDRIS rocket whirled slowly in deep space around the Lost Planet. Inside the deceased crew members slept unaware of the iridescent dark red orb hurling towards them. The red orb struck the rocket and blasted it into the vacuum of space.

XIII.　　The Fall of the Seven

Without the Salvs, the Luminist Council convened in the Temple of the Telemesca. Only Opian Lums were permitted entry, along with common Opians who had exclusive warrants for their presence. Various ministers and their assistants were crowding around Minister Seleyis, the elder Lum emissary to the Salvs, replacing the late Master Serjo. "IDRIS-10 is lost! Along with Zaxxon-II and the METRIS rover!" Master Lindra exclaimed. Master Ojiri's divis were twitching wildly as he shouted above the commotion. "Will they retaliate if we halt our Searine herb production?" Many of the Lum councilors coiled their divis angrily in agreement. Something had to be done.

"Have they enslaved extrasalvine life on other planets?" Master Jabulon, Councilor of the largest tribe, the Baali said.   "What will they do if we land the Zaxxon satellite on the Lost Planet?" Master Niris asked trying to speak above the Baali Councilor. "Is it true they know beings from other worlds have visited Salv?" Jabulon said. "Why do they make us their psi-slaves?" He continued indignantly. Jabulon was one of the most influential on the Luminist Council, next Masters Junal and Niris, alongside the Emissary Seleyis.

The Telemesca priests murmured among themselves quietly. Their oracles knew dangerous times approached. The twenty-two priests chosen for life had recurrent nightmares of the Floating Monoliths and the prophecies of their unbelievable transformation. "The loss of the IDRIS-10 space mission is inconceivable. To think that the Salvs caused the deaths of Opian rocketeers and the loss of our machines is unthinkable. Yet it did happen and we have no explanation from them or the Seven." Master Niris began. Several of the Lums nodded and writhed their divis in consensus. Master Junal spoke up. "We have no way to substantiate Salv interference with the IDRIS-10 mission." Master Jaanah slid his divis around in agreement. "We must take into account that during the past alignment, the Patho Council informed us all diagnoses of the Rencis Pandemic and Mnemositis have been cured." Jaanah addressed the Council. Opian Pathos (Patho, the professional title for Lum healers) reported all cases of the terminal Rencis and Mnemositis diseases cured within the last alignment (a period of three Terran months on Salv measured by Salvs and Opians).

Lums in the Scientific Assembly murmured their own theories, all centered on the Salvs. "Master Jaanah, we also cannot corroborate Salv involvement with the Rencis and Mnemositis phenomenon." Master Ojiri said. "Camarilla intervention in our society is this Council's simplest hypothesis as an explanation of recent phenomena is more likely veritable than other available hypothesis. The Baali councilor Master Jabulon said above the others. The Lum Council quieted their clamor, listening to Jabulon. "I concur." Master Junal said after a while, twisting and uncoiling his divis pensively. "Among competing hypotheses, Camarilla interference in Opian culture makes the fewest assumptions. This hypothesis should be selected, and acted on." The Council was quiet save for a few murmurs of agreement as Jabulon continued.

"You use that term liberally Master Jabulon. Opian civilization has greatly benefited from the vital philosophic and technological intelligence of the Salvs. What is the basis of our theories about the Camarilla?" Master Niris said. "Our coexistence with the Salvs has never been violent. The first Covenant Gathering between the Lum tribes and the Seven was over a thousand conjunctions ago. During the Period of the

Derobion Wars the Seven first approached the Telemesca oracles. Cycles later the Salvs held conclaves with the High Priest of the Kataan, and the Coridian monks." Niris continued. Jabulon's divis coiled and uncoiled in disagreement. *When the Baali governed the Luminist Council, Opian civilization experienced no incidents at the divis of the Salvs. We launched into space with the first rocketeers, and found our own vaccines for Edoxis* he thought. Jabulon kept his thoughts to himself, though he knew the Baali and other Councilors concurred with him.

"Yet at no time in the history of our civilization have the Camarilla interfered in our wars or space missions." Master Junal addressed Jabulon directly. The Opian Lum flashed his red eyes and coiled his divis indignantly at Junal. "Noninterference on the Salvs account is logical, Master Junal. Foster the degeneration of Opian civilization. Maintain our divisions over Searine production while they live in their secret biodomes far on the outskirts of our Vils. Restrict access to their vital centres of religion. Salvs do not even communicate with us!" Jabulon could see many of the Lum Councilors writhe their divis in consensus.

Several Lum Councilors again began taking at once, clamoring above each other's voices. "I propose we decrease Searine crystallization by seventy percent." Jabulon raised his voice above the commotion. "I motion for a formal poll to assemble a delegation to contravene the Seven's edicts." Many of the Baali Lums and Opians held their divis up above their head as customary shows of solidarity. Master Junal, already coiling his divis in disapproval, let out an audible hiss. "Master Ojiri will poll the Scientific Assembly on the IDRIS-11 mission. Then we will proceed with Master Jabulon's poll." Master Seleyis remained silent, his head lowered and divis sliding slowly around his arms and shoulders in deep concentration.

Seleyis noticed several of the Councilors looking at him with various expressions and divi gestures. He could feel their fear over Jabulon's Baali influence, as much as he felt the majority of Lums voicing their reserved outrage and fear. Jabulon was quickly becoming the voice and face of their silent outrage and distress. He noticed Master Junal preparing to speak and acknowledge him. Seleyis could feel Junal's vital force concentrating on him, his name resonant in Junal's mind. Finally, he could remain silent no longer.

"Our katras are linked with the fate of the Salvs. Our civilization does not understand this now, nor do I." Seleyis said. Ojiri and Lindra twisted their divis in a sign of non-verbal agreement. "Our civilization has only possessed the capability of orbital launch for three conjunctions. Many tribal confederacies are still in states of armed conflicts. Salvs only confirmed the existence of extrasalvine life during the era of the Coridian Governance of the Lum Council. We have no program of geo-engineering, where we tap the thermal energy of the Golam volcanoes and exploit the cyclonic energy of aklons, nor are we able to extract the tensile energy of planetary quakes. Technology the Salvs have offered us." Seleyis was mainly addressing Jabulon.

"But no….we are forbidden to land on Lost Planet. Now *all* our Zaxxon series satellites have been destroyed. What is the Seven hiding on the Lost One? They dispense technological enterprise to us at their bidding. Why have they forbidden access to their bioships or psionic technology? Why do they remain on this planet silently meditating, with no attempts at interaction?" Jabulon countered. *I cannot speak of their mysteries or transcendent intelligences. The ships of light I felt burned into my mind, the engineering of entire extrasalvine civilizations and worlds shatters my thoughts into troubling images I could never transfer into words.* Seleyis thought.

"We must poll the Council and ascertain whether a contravention is logical. The IDRIS incident must not go unrequited." Master Lindra said. The Council adjourned the session, polling within the Scientific Assembly and Luminists. The Assembly poll gave overwhelming support for the IDRIS-11 next alignment. Master Jabulon conducted his poll on the measure of response to the IDRIS disaster and Salv interference in the Mnemositis and Rencis pestilences. The Luminist Council polled nearly two-thirds in favor of a measured contravention. The three-cycle session concluded with final orations from the Lums Masters.

"The Council has disregarded a serious matter during recent incidents. The tribal confederacies of Misraam have again attacked Kataanese settlements on the borders of Baali and the Hira confederacies." Master Jabulon addressed the Luminists. "I concur. For nearly ten alignments, the Misraam attacks have occurred without Luminist sanction. Misraam has forbidden proctors from the Scientific Assembly to inspect their missile installations." Lindra said.

The Misraam, Hira, and Baali Lums all began speaking and protesting at once. Master Jabulon twisted his divis in satisfaction. Junal attempted repeated to speak above the disorder. Suddenly as quickly as the commotion started, Lums grew silent in groups throughout the Telemesca Temple as a lone Lum made his way to the assembly platform. Kwai bowed ceremoniously to the Lum Masters.

The lone survivor of the IDRIS-10 disaster waited for permission to speak. Kwai looked over at his father, Junal, noticing his father's disapproval at his presence in the amphitheater and obvious concern over his physical condition. "Kwai-sii. You honor this

Council with your bravery in the face of disaster. Should you not be convalescing in your biodome?" Master Jabulon greeted him affectionately. "Kwai-sii…" Junal began, but Kwai interrupted raising his divis above his head with his hands, in an old Baali tribal display of solidarity. The Baali Lums and their confederated tribes cheered loudly. Jabulon smiled at the display and motioned for silence. "Father…Masters…I come here to speak of the events surrounding the disaster. I feel what I must say should be said to this Council and not in an official LUMSCIEX testimony." He said weakly, his divis wrapped protectively around him. "Within an arc-cycle of deploying the METRIS rover, we were attacked by the Salvs." Seleyis lowered his head and coiled his divis gently. The Council roared.

Kwai and Tura sat with Junal in the old Lum's biodome one alignment after his address to the Council. "My advisement to the IDRIS-11 mission is complete father. I have refused formal acceptance as a mission proctor. My presence will remain advisory during the launch." Junal's divis twisted apprehensively. "Seti reports to LUMSCIEX command center next alignment. She is under the tutelage of Seleyis who has nominated her to be initiated into the Council." Kwai and Tura looked at their father, surprised. "A female? On the Council!" Tura exclaimed. "The mission to the Lost One will be dangerous. Tura and I must have counsel with her and Master Seleyis." Tura glanced at his sibling. He knew Kwai's intentions to help organize the Salv contravention.

"This will be the last mission in several alignments. The Baali are threatening to halt all crystallization of Searine, and the Kataans are massing along the Coridian territories, threatening to intervene in the Misraam-Hira conflict." Junal informed his matured sons. "Make precautions in your transports to

LUMSCIEX. The Council has not ruled out the possibility of Misraam and Baali subterfuge." "We will make precautions. Tura and I will go to counsel with Master Seleyis and Seti. I will accompany here to LUMSCIEX. " Kwai said. Junal twisted his divis slowly. "I transport to the Baali capital Vil, to help them organize a convention at the biodomes of the Seven." Tura said. "Kwai will join me after the IDRIS mission." "Proceeding with this mission could have unforeseen consequences that could affect our entire civilization." Junal replied, his divis curling around his shoulders.

The next cycle, Kwai and Tura set out for Master Seleyis' biodome. Thousands of Weeping Triphylloid and phylo plants of iridescent colors writhed and wiggled, chuckling and baying all around the Vil where Seleyis' biodome sat on the outskirts secluded. Glowing blue and green vapors floated in a haze, illuminating the landscape. In the distance, living Weeping Triphylloids heckled, swaying wildly at the approaching Lums.

A Howling Zephyrid swooped down on a stumbling Tetrog, shrieking its recognizable screech as the large predatory avian beast dove in on the wounded Tetrog. Before the Zephyrid's gaping spiked maw could envelop the poor Tetrog, a towering Cephaloyte sloth whipped its slimy tongues out, snatching the Tetrog away from the Zephyrid. The avian Zephyrid crashed into the ground fatally as the Cephaloyte sloth wiggled on its way. A swarm of Irak scavengers quickly swooped in from the indigo haze, carrying off the ill-fated Zephyrid for their meal.

Kwai and Tura hurried though the artificially lit pathway leading up to the entrance of Seleyis' biodome. A customary bowl of fruits left out for passersby was partially consumed. As was socially accustomed for Opian Lums, Master Seleyis' door was open, as Kwai and Tura announced their presence formally. Receiving no response, they hesitated in the threshold of the Lum biodome. Tura looked at Kwai and hissed quietly, coiling his divis protectively. Kwai repeated the gesture carefully. Suddenly Tura's red eyes flashed white then back to red, as the dotted blue patterns on his green skin turned violet. Tura felt his entire skin tingle, as if it was vibrating. His divis reacted to a sudden wave of sensual pleasure, emitting vaporous fluidic mist. The Lum began to convulse and collapsed to the ground letting out an involuntary moan.

Kwai grabbed his sibling and pulled his hands back in pain from the electric pulse he received. "Tura…" he hissed. Kwai attempted to clutch Tura again slowly by the arms, the electric pulse weak enough to cause only a minor shock. Kwai helped him up to a sitting position. Tura's divis were undulating wildly. Their minds were envisioning thoughts that did not originate in their Opian brains. Their eyes flashed pale red and white, stinging from the vapors that filled the biodome. The vapors formed a luminous indigo haze inside. Confused and frightened, the Lums strained to think clearly, hearing a faint pulsating hum coming from Master Seleyis' study.

Kwai and Tura heard a symphony of melodic voices in their minds. A refrain of voices echoed in their thoughts, speaking as one. *Gaze into the Lattice.* Thought-forms entered Kwai and Tura's mind, of the cosmic expanse, and thousands of vast alien civilizations. Their flashing red and white eyes began to sting as their vision became blurred. Slowly they walked with serious effort towards Seleyis' study. A vaporous trail of luminous indigo mist floated all around inside the biodome, originating from Seleyis' large study-chamber.

The voluminous study chamber was dimly lit with candlelight, as the two Lums heard a loud pulsing hum. Tura and Kwai shouted in disbelief and anger at the fantastic sight before them. Juuri, Seti and Seleyis' sat in meditation, a red meditation sphere materialized a few meters above each of them. Their ethereal katra bodies projected and formed within the meditation spheres. Sitting on the other side of the shadowy study chamber were the Salvs Zoroa and Zeb. The two Salvs were conjoined, morphing, and melding into bizarre forms. Tura and Kwai had witnessed the bizarre site before during their last encounter with Salvs at Seleyis' biodome under similar circumstances.

Kwai shouted at the meditating group. "We are not Camarilla psi-slaves!" Tura was disoriented, staring in horror at the morphing Salvs, changing in shape and size, their dark red and indigo skin flashing with luminous spiraling patterns of color. Kwai heard the hive of symphonic voices inside his mind. Leave in amity. *Before you have separated the katra…you cannot know that what is seen outside the spheres does not exist.*

Kwai reeled at the strange voices and their bizarre message. The two frightened Lums then heard a familiar voice enveloped in their consciousness, a voice that was not a voice bringing words to thought forms. *Kwai. Tura. You must go in peace. We are assembling with the Seven.* Seti voiced to them clairvoyantly.

Tura was confused and terrified. *What in the name of my katra is ….* Before he could complete his labored thought, Tura heard Seti telepathically communicate with him and Kwai again. *They are dying.* Kwai looked at Tura and knew his sibling heard the same message. Did Seti mean the Salvs, or was she relaying the voice of the Hive, referring to Opians? Tura abruptly rushed toward Seti and Seleyis grabbing them. The beings in the chamber all became disoriented at once. The five Lums became disoriented at once in a terrible clamor.

The red meditation spheres hovering above Seti and Seleyis dissipated along with their ethereal bodies encased inside. The physical bodies of Juuri, Seti, and Seleyis collapsed to the floor in disorientation. All five Lums experienced a violent painful electric pulse, knocking all four to the floor in disoriented pain. Juuri hissed in anguish. Zoroa and Zeb's morphing meld immediately ceased, as the two Salvs instantly reverted to their original forms, towering nearly a dozen meters above the four Opians on the floor.

Zoroa and Zeb slid their divis along Seleyis, Juuri's, and Seti's shorter divis, connecting them. Glowing blue fluidic light flowed down through Salvs divis into the unconscious Lums divis and around their heads. Kwai regained his footing and helped Tura up.

The two drew their benta shafts and started towards the Salvs. The shafts quickly flew out of their hands, slamming into the wall. Tura let out a hiss of surprise. Regaining their posture, the Lums quickly backed out of Seleyis' study, and ran out of the biodome. Tura groaned and hissed at his childhood companion.

"It is the Camarilla. We must go to Master Jabulon." Kwai said. "The Council has become incapacitated by Camarilla apologists, and the Misraam-Hira conflict. Only the Baali can lead any contravention against the Salvs, and protect us." Tura grabbed his friend to support himself. "The spheres, what are they Kwai?" "Salv psionic weapons. The phenomenon appears to be some sort of particle containment that amplifies neural pulses from our brains into the divis, somehow projecting ghostly manifestations of our katras." Kwai explained. Such a weapon could harness neural energy, as a focused wave. Similar to the orb of energy that destroyed METRIS and IDRIS-10.

I knew it was the Salvs. Kwai thought. As he and Tura started walking down the esplanade, Kwai turned to his sibling, "Tura. Go to the Baali consulate and remain with Master Jabulon until the IDRIS-11 mission is complete." Kwai instructed his sibling. *I must speak with Seleyis and the Salvs.* Kwai thought, wondering if Seti and Seleyis knew his deliberations. "IF the Salvs are proselytizing Seti, I must speak with her about the IDRIS-11 mission. I will not leave Juuri." "We will organize the contravention." Tura said. Tura departed, continuing on his way. He still felt disoriented, but capable of walking. Tura's thoughts did not feel as if they originated in his own mind. He felt like his consciousness was in a haze of euphoria.

Confused, Tura's body remained physically stimulated. An unfamiliar sensation surrounded his mind. Tura began to feel a need to be in the presence of a Salv. The Salv transferences were beyond any sensual pleasure he had experienced in life. He needed to touch a Salv, touch their undulating divis, each having different spiraling, and dotted patterns along the entire length of them.

The anxious Opian made his way down the esplanade. Weeping Triphylloids, cackling Zephytrope plants and dozens of other bioluminescent whirling plants, opening and closing, growing and shrinking into various petals and stems, and All sorts of harmonious chortling from the Phylos, Crawling Crystal Yarite rocks twittered as strange spotted yellow Polyps floated above him.

In Seleyis' biodome, Seti sat in silence with Master Seleyis. Zoroa and Zeb had projected a holographic plasma display of their ancient religious ceremonies used during the Great Soliloquy of Zejiss'ajra at the Third Soliloquy of Convergence. The two Opian Lums sat listening to the Salvs use their ancient melodic language in harmonic conjunction.

The Salvs dissolved the fluidic hologram and gazed down at Seleyis and Seti. The Seven is in danger. The Time of the Tear is with us. Seleyis and Seven felt the Hive voice resound within their consciousness. *The Sleeping is coming soon. Make no attempts to land on the Lost One.* Seti felt the Hive symphony echo within her mind. *I will make the landing. Not as a part of the contravention precious one, no…to bring our civilizations together in katra.* She voiced back to the Seven.

The ethereal katra depends upon the passions, and especially of sensuality, purging the lower emotions of physical compulsions makes the katra receptive to the vital-intelligences of all living katras in the universe. Zeb voiced to the Opians, listening to their discourse. *Katra is an effusion of light upon it, the unifying lattice that holds all life forms in the whirling nexus of realities. Through its means are effused the illuminations of our sciences upon the created worlds.* Seleyis and Seti saw their thought-forms visualize within the Hive mind inside their consciousness. Zeb's divis danced fantastically around his body flashing brilliant glowing patterns. Zoroa continued the transference.

Thus is explained the name given to Opians by their Telemesca, Illuminant, *which Salvs call* Camarilla. *The Lattices were originally lit from the Light of the Supernal Katra. The degrees and orders of intelligent beings and their katras of light do not ascend in an infinite series, but rise to a final Intelligent Design, the NOOR who is Light in and by Itself, upon which comes no light from any external source, the nexus of the Universe, from where every light is effused into the Katra of all living life-forms…*Seleyis and Seti curled and uncurled their undulating divis, immersed in ten-thousand light years of Salvic knowledge.

When the conscious state of the living Katra prevails, it is called in relation to a being who experiences it, illuminance, Extinction of Extinction, for the Katra has become transcendent to itself, extinct to its own extinction; it becomes unconscious of Being and unconscious of its own unconsciousness. The illuminant Being immersed in this state is called NOORI in the language of reality, Unification. In the nexus of the NOORI are the spiraling verities of the cosmic expanse. The Salvs suddenly stopped the transference, and began to rise from their meditative sitting posture. Seleyis looked at Seti. "There is danger here…you must go Seti-sii…now." *Remain. Precious ones. We will adjourn.* Zoroa and Zeb voiced with the Hive telepathically to Seleyis, Juuri, and Seti. The Salvs quickly exited the biodome and set out towards the approaching menace they could feel pulsating with fear and contempt.

Kwai strode hurriedly down the esplanade of orchards outside the Vil leading back to Seleyis' biodome. His own kindred, psi-slave to the Camarilla! Seleyis must answer to the Council, and his Katra willing, the Baali would assume control of the Council through the next elective poll. Luminist Councilors were appointed for life, yet their successors were elected each conjunction to prevent unnecessary interruptions in government when a Councilor did become deceased. Nearly a dozen of the Luminists were approaching the end of their expected lifespans, including his father, Master Junal.

Kwai stopped in his tracks, in sight of the two approaching Salvs Zoroa, and Zeb. He touched the recording device on his handheld communicator, attempting to capture his interaction with the Salvs. Within arc-cycles of switching the recording command, his device lost all power, going dark. Zoroa and Zeb walked up to him, towering over the startled Opian

Lum by nearly a dozen meters high. Their deep red and indigo skin tone contrasted with his light green and patterned blue skin. *Peace be with you and in your Katra.* Kwai heard their melodic voices echo telepathically within his own consciousness.

"Speak aurally!" Kwai shouted at them. *Why can you not quiet the anger and fear in your mind? Speak with your Katra precious one. We will listen.* He felt the aural voices singing inside his mind but could not hear them. "We are not your Searine targs, or psi-slaves. Opians have never known freedom under the Salv Camarilla!" Kwai stepped closer to the Salvs, circling around them. He sensed something, something that was a small, an ethereal scent. A smell he could not put into words or even begin cognitive description of what he could smell. He could smell a strange presence in the air around the Salvs as he circled.

The air around them was becoming strange, luminescent, and fluidic. *Fear. They are afraid.* No, not fear…remorse…despair…a deep desolation …. loneliness …they are dying! Kwai exclaimed to himself. As soon as he came to this revelation, he observed the Salv's slowly twist and slide their divis upward from the length of their tall lithe bodies.

"We will be free of your elitist plot!" Kwai shouted at them again, raising his divis slowly above his head in aggression and a customary Opian gesture of solidarity within a tribe. *Precious one. Your sister Seti-sii is in great peril in her quest to set foot onto the Lost One. This will imperil her entire crew and your entire civilization.* Kwai could feel pulsating sensations in his divis; his mind could not formulate cogent thoughts anymore. Then everything happened and Opian history changed forever.

Kwai felt his divis begin to sting with a warm fluidic sensation that prompted physical arousal from him. He was becoming disoriented, beginning to feel..to feel..feel…what *was* he feeling? He could not think..he needed..needed..what *was* it? He needed. He did not know what. *Need..I need..I need..to touch..* Kwai started towards Zeb as he circled around the Salvs, confused, his mind in a dysfunctional haze. He reached out and grabbed Zeb's divi an instant before the Salv could lash it away from him.

Zeb let out a loud hiss, flashing his eyes from gold to pale white. He lashed the divi back and forth; causing Kwai to lose his grip and fall to the ground hard. Kwai grunted and pulled out his benta shaft, diving towards the Salv. Lurching upright, Kwai plunged the plasma end of the benta shaft into Zeb's divi.

Zeb let out a sibilant shriek causing the living phylo plants around him to twitter and cackle loudly. Zoroa quickly coiled up her divis, and placed her hands on Zeb attempting to heal him quickly with cellular regeneration. Kwai raised the benta plasma shaft high above his head, lurching towards Zoroa's mid torso. Before he could land a blow, he felt the benta shaft fly out of his hands landing dozens of meters away.

'Zeb's voice cascaded into his consciousness, splitting his mind. *Precious one. Cease this! Seti is in...* Hearing his sibling's name, Kwai lunged again at Zeb's divis that swiftly coiled around his hands. Kwai was pulled a dozen meters up by his hands to the Salv's face.

Kwai was becoming faint, his own divis burning unbearably. Feeling himself on the verge of losing consciousness, he summoned the last reserves of his strength and kicked the Salv in his eye with all his force. Zeb's eyes flashed pale white in pain, releasing his divis coiled around Kwai's hands, and dropping him back down to the ground. Landing hard, Kwai rolled over onto his back and sat up slowly. *Zeb we must flee from the mad Opian.* Zoroa voiced silently, conveying her concern. Seti has not fled the biodome. They are not safe. Zeb voiced back to her. Zeb and Zoroa clairvoyantly projected the peril around Seleyis, warning them to flee. *Precious Seleyis-sii...Seti-sii...Juuri-sii* their psionic bond abruptly ended as they saw Kwai remove his blaster from the side of his utility sash and point it at them.

As quickly as he removed the plasma blaster and aimed it, Kwai was hurled backwards by an invisible force. The telekinetic psi-blast knocked the blaster from him as he landed five meters away beneath a Weeping Triphylloid. The living plant towered above him, bending its stem down to leer at him.

The plant wrapped its long vines around his throat, causing him to retch. He struggled to loosen the Triphylloid's grip around his throat, watching the Salvs tower over him with concern. He heard a strange whistling sound and hiss come from Zeb. The Weeping Triphylloid's vine around his throat tightened then began to loosen, as his consciousness faded. The last thing he saw clearly was the look of horror and shock on Zoroa's face as a plasma blast burst through her chest.

Tura fired again. This time at Zeb, hitting the Salv in both his divis. Shrieking in pain and shock, Zeb stumbled away from Zoroa, his tattered and shredded divi causing him to fall to the ground. Tura had used crystallized Searine to hide his biological and psionic imprint from the Salvs. Baali scientists had successfully discovered that the crystallization of Searine when implanted into an Opian Lum's divis caused them to remain undetected by the Salv's powerful clairvoyance.

Tura walked over to the fallen Salv, Zoroa and fired several shots at her divis, causing her to writhe in pain. He unsheathed his benta shaft and sunk it into Zoroa's chest, watching her eyes turn from golden to white, and then dark indigo as the life drained from the Salv.

Zeb stood up in pain , as he began the exhaustive process to regenerate the damaged cells on his divis. He knew it would take several long cycles to heal fully. Zeb nearly collapsed again in unbearable physical agony and psychological distress. The life had drained from Zoroa, one of the Seven who counseled Salv civilization. Zeb fled before the Opian could inflict fatal damage. Never before in the history of Opian and Salv civilizations had an Opian ever mortally wounded a Salv.

The Seven was breached. The entire ancient covenant between Opian Lums and Salvs was contravened. Tura walked over to his unconscious friend and moved him away from the Weeping Triphylloid. A symphony of wailing and all manners of hissing, cackling, and other commotion assailed their divi senses.

The indigo night howled as myriads of floating beasts, twisting and cackling plants rang out sounds of despair that would astonish most humanoid auditory nerves. Crawling Crystal Yarite rocks shattered from the nocturnal Salvic symphony. Salvs all across the planet slowly swathed their divis around their dark red bodies in remorse and in honor.

Zevyla, Zilah, Zsiji, Zenobia, Zephyra, and Savene who were the remainder of the former Seven undulated and twisted their divis solemnly in a regal ritual ten thousand years old on Salv. The six Salv guides began to sing the Great Soliloquy of Zoroa. They clasped hands and divis, raising them high toward the Lost Planet.

XIV.   LANDING

The Luminist Council was in session in the Lum central amphitheater. There were no Salvs present as Master Ojiri addressed the Council. "Considering the situation with the Salvs, Seti has agreed to remain in the IDRIS-11 space mission. Proctor Jaxoon will command the mission, Jadiss will pilot the IDRIS, Jubila, Jubilum, and Jachin will serve the mission as the remaining crew compliment." Opians murmured and whispered quietly as Master Ojiri read the crew roster. Many of the rocketeers like Jaxoon, and Jubilum were well known in Opian infos.

"Master Ojiri has LUMSCIEX organized contingency operations for the mission?" Master Lindra asked. "Lord Joaz has Spiden Zed-77 fighter-rockets patrolling the mesosphere around the orbital launch perimeter. Once IDRIS achieves geosynchronous orbit the crew will deploy the new Tetis-Zed communications array which will synchronize with the Icon-II satellite in order to reinforce planetary communications to IDRIS." Master Jabulon nodded at Ojiri and stood to address the rest of the Council.

"Masters, the Misraam-Hira war has spread into the borders of the Kataan. We are now seeing the consequences of inaction and unwarranted economic oppression by the Kataan. In consideration of this historic mission, the Baali will not provoke the conflict and place our legions on alert. If the situation remains unchanged after the mission and the safety of the crew is determined…." Dozens of Hira and Misraam Opians began shouting and protesting all out once at the Baali Lum. "Baali Lums occupied the Hira tribal provinces for over 100 alignments! But this…" Master Jodol, the Lum representing the large Kataan tribe interrupted

Jabulon. The Baali Councilor lash his divis in the direction of Jodol, a severe insult for an Opian Lum. Jabulon countered, interrupting Jodol before he could finish. " But no...Kataanese have halted Searine production by seventy percent. We Baali are forced to compensate for the disparity after providing securities in Phylax to the Coridian tribes."

The Baali Opians in the amphitheater shouted in support, audibly drowning out the protesting Misraam and Hira Opians. "Now inconsequentially, Phylax does not compensate for Searine. Yet it was Baali engineers who successfully tested the first Searine crystallization into the Red Vapor." Jabulon continued. "Red Vapor is forbidden. It is against all tribal treaties to produce the compound." Master Jaanah interrupted sternly.

Jabulon continued. "Red Vapor is what the Salvs use to power their bioships and our scientists have observed the Seven using Red Vapor in an altered form for some manner of religious ritual." Master Jodol rose again, moved to stand near Niris and Jaanah, addressing his fellow Kataan Lums. He knew he could count on the Coridian logic of Junal to prevent the conflict from widening.

"Master Jabulon informed us of Lord Joaz's strategic coordination in case the mission is threatened. We must for the time being, and for the sake of all Opians, present a unified defense strategy in case the Salvs threaten the mission and the crew." Jabulon curled his divis in reluctant agreement with Jodol. *Even though I would rather see the Kataanese fool blasted into atoms, he is right.* He said to himself. "This Council must consider all contingencies, including unthinkable scenarios. Lord Joaz has met with the Lords of all the tribal legions. The majority of Legionnaires and other Lum military chiefs concur we must implement the Nexus Command, in case of grave threat to our civilization from the Salvs or any unforeseen threat from Lost Planet." The amphitheater quieted except for the murmurs of a few Lums who were old enough to know the consequences of atomic warfare if the Nexus Command was used.

Junal and Seleyis slowly twisted their divis and uncurled them down their bodies. The Command would the strategic defense congress consisting of the military heads of Opian tribes that a grave threat existed on such a level that Opian civilization was in peril from the Salvs. Atomic weapons were used by Opian legions twice in Opian history. The Baali air legions launched atomic weapons at the Derobion tribe Vils of Dhainu and Oreb seventy conjunctions ago. Radioactive fallout lingered in the affected areas since the detonations, as Opian genetic aberrations only recently subsided.

"I propose we poll the Council on whether the authority should be granted to issue the Nexus Command on the premise of its principles to protect Opian society from grave peril." Jabulon said. "The Nexus Command would only be issued by unanimous consensus in the Council. Lord Joaz would then issue a security protocol to the tribal legions possessing the launch systems." Jodol said. Seleyis could listen no more, and stood up to address the Council.

"I must protest. The Salvs have never harmed an Opian. The recent incidents occurred as two Salvs, one of them a Seven, were attacked by two Opians who in no way would understand the meditations of Seti and I." Seleyis' voice strained. *Kwai and Tura's interruption in the meditations with the Salvs caused the transference to terminate prematurely, the fools nearly caused permanent neural damage.* "Master Seleyis, why did you not advise the Council of your continuing meditations with the Salvs, especially with a Salv who was one of the Seven?" Jabulon said sharply. "If we are to entrust you as Master Serpo's successor as Emissary to the Seven, how can we trust you if you do not inform us of your interactions with them?" Opians in all tribes throughout the chamber all waved their divis in agreement, murmuring loudly.

"My protégé was approached several times by Salvs. Her mental abilities are significantly advanced, more than the average Lum. She has already experienced several transferences. Her abilities and scientific expertise allowed her a seat on this mission." Seleyis faced Jabulon. Before he could continue, Ojiri interrupted them. "Reports from our anthropologists reveal that the Salvs are planning some sort of mass event, possibly an exodus from the planet." Seleyis turned to face the rest of the Luminist Council, sliding his divis slowly around him.

"We must not fear beings we do not understand. We have only begun to unlock the mind's potential. We have yet to learn how to regenerate the natural resources of Salv, its vast seas, and climatic diversity. One cycle far into the stories of our thirdchildren, we will build ships and look to the stars. We will tell them, we are travelling with our Salv brothers and sisters, and meeting wondrous beings. We will tell our descendants that war is a stain on the katras of all Opians. Conjunctions from now, we will tell our thirdchildren Opians and Salvs lifted their eyes to the stars together." Many Opians and Lums in the amphitheater raised their divis as high as possible, flashing their eyes from dark to light red in show of praise. They would echo and retell his speech to their children and thirdchildren for many generations.

"That was a very touching oration Master Seleyis-zan. Inspiring. Unfortunately, we must recognize the issues at hand, wars will not solve themselves. Baali are being threatened and killed daily by Kataanese in the Misraam-Hira war." Hundreds of Baali Opians raised and waved their divis as Jabulon countered Seleyis' speech. "If Kataanese do not withdraw from Misraam and Hira, Baali have no choice but to defend our tribal confederate interests." Jodol scoffed at Jabulon's ultimatum. *If Baali want war then we will prepare for it. Over our dead bodies will we allow the Baali Empire to rise again. Never again.* Jodol thought. The Luminist Council polled their Councilors who overwhelmingly voiced support for the Nexus Command authority to be activated allowing Opian legions a nuclear reaction to any perceived threat to the IDRIS-11 mission or Opian civilization.

Kwai and Tura had reported their attack and death of the Salv Zoroa to the Luminist Council a few cycles after the incident. Before the session, the Lum Masters unanimously agreed to exclude the Seven from any future sessions until Seleyis and other Masters contacted the Salvs after the IDRIS-11 mission.

Kwai and Tura's account greatly interested Master Jabulon who offered amnesty and a safe haven in the Baali tribe at his biodomes. Jabulon was wealthy and owned three biodomes. Kwai set out to LUMSCIEX three cycles before the IDRIS launch while Tura remained with the Baali, assisting them in diplomatic efforts to end the Misraam-Hira war. Seti refused to see her two mature siblings.

Master Junal sat with Seti in his biodome before she departed to prepare for the IDRIS mission. "Seti-sii. What do you expect to find on Lost Planet? What have you learned from the Salvs during your transferences?" Junal asked his child. Seti lowered her head and twisted her divis thoughtfully. "The mind is where all the wonders of science and imagination begin. It is as limitless as the vacuum of space, where all mysteries begin and end. The mind is the nexus of all mysteries, and wonders, and scientific discovery. Salvs have explored the mind and its vital-force to the depths of our katras. They learned to harvest the universe father." Junal held his daughters hands in his.

No matter what happens on that world....no matter what you see Seti...I will be there with you." "I know father." Seti said, wiping her father's tears away.

A few cycles later, the launch control center at LUMSCIEX, the Luminist Scientific Exploration Division bustled with activity. The rocket crew led by Proctor Jaxoon and Jubilum sat in their command pods inside the rocket. Seti and the other crewmembers waiting in their spacesuits for the control center to conduct a final command poll to authorize the historic launch. The launch rocket engineers, communications engineers, Environment advisors, all began to advise the IDRIS Mission Proctor on the safety and security of launching the IDRIS rocket.

"Launch Communications Array to Mission Proctor." A communications officer opened the central comm-links to the launch control center and the Ion-powered rocket. "Mission Proctor, go ahead Array." "Proctor you have a clear link to begin the mission poll." "Recognized, Array. Security Protocol. Advise Proctor, are there any abstentions to proceed?" "Security Protocol. No abstentions on the mission at this time." "Recognized. Patho Homoeopathic Proctor." "Ay, Proceed. No abstentions." "Retrofuel and Recovery Proctor." "Ay, proceed." "Ion Drive Control." "Ay." "SCIEX Jibiru Juno Control Center." "Ay." "Febula Data Network Station." "Ay all systems proceed." "Flight Telemetry and Guidance." "Ay." "Comm Array Proctor." "Ay, all networks on-link." "IDRIS Proctor. SCIEX." "SCIEX. IDRIS Proctor and crew report no abstentions. Proceed." "Jibiru Juno Control. IDRIS Mission Proctor. Our mission sector confirms no abstentions to launch. Launch is so. Recognize." "SCIEX. Jibiru Juno Control. Recognize." The crew sealed their space helmets preparing to launch. Seti flashed her eyes letting her thoughts echo into the Salv mind-hive.

The journey has begun. Precious ones, you know of what was in the beginning and the journey without end. Consecrate our katras to Noor, forgive our errant bodies for we only wish to walk among the stars with you. Seti voiced telepathically as the launch countdown began. She could feel the entire Hivemind's harmonic symphony within her entire katra. *The Sleep is coming. Prepare precious ones.* For an instant in time, Seti's mind was the Salv Hive, and she felt their profound transcendent sadness. Would they be waiting for her on the Lost Planet? The pod communicator roused her out of her meditation. "IDRIS. SCIEX Jibiru Juno. Mission Proctor confirms launch is so." "SCIEX. IDRIS. Recognized. Launch is so. We will meet you on dataslip Jax 1-zed." "IDRIS. SCIEX. To the stars and into the void. Honor to you as you honor us all, our never-ending journey and search for ourselves has just begun." "Recognize ay ay." Proctor Jaxoon said into his pod communicator. "We take the hands of all Opians and begin this journey together. Let's go and not stop until we've set foot on strange worlds and cast our eyes to Salv." Jaxoon's transmission would be told by Opian zooda and transzooda Proctors to their students for generations.

"IDRIS. SCIEX Juno CC. Launch in Count-set 70 arcs…." "SCIEX. IDRIS. Recognized. 70 arcs…." Jaxoon instructed the crew to prepare for launch via his interlink communicator. Jubila monitored the flight telemetry controls and plasma gauges. All systems and ion engine drives were operational; there were no indication of constraints. "30 arcs…" LUMSCIEX launch proctors communicated the final stage of the launch countdown. "25 arcs…20 arcs…7 arcs…" The rockets ion engines whined and roared, emitting a long trail of blue and white plasma behind the rocket as it blasted off, hurling through the indigo atmosphere.

Three cycles after the IDRIS rocket launch, the crew diligently entered in computer commands in their respective pods that would begin the separated command lander's slow descent onto the surface of the Lost Planet. Separation from the main rocket had gone smoothly as the command module Opians named "Catarina" detached and began descending into the Lost Planet's atmosphere.

Engineer Jachin verified his calculations to Proctor Jaxoon, confirming the command module began its descent from geosynchronous orbit. "Proctor Jaxoon, descent confirmed from 7.131 degrees zenith over Lost Planet. Descent thermosphere insertion PAD 314.101 Mu. Velocity 71 -00757. Set perigee zed 00078 00753 017 007 293." "Recognized, Jachin. Set perigee descent. Return to block Zed-33, and realign to thermo insert. Standby for ion ignition." Jaxoon commanded as the rocket entered the thermosphere of the Lost Planet.

"Mark 700 arcs for plasma thrust. SCIEX Juno. IDRIS. Recognize ion ignition for plasma thrust on my mark." Jaxoon communicated with SCIEX Mission Control in the Opian Vil of Jibiru-Juno. "IDRIS. SCIEX Juno. Recognize mark, Jaxoon." "Ignite. Pitch 007 Jadiss. I am on dataslip 17-zed." "Recognized. Ignition is so." The pilot Jadiss replied to Proctor Jaxoon. "IDRIS SCIEX Juno. Tetis-Zed array reads you well. Jaxoon, all communications now synchronized with Icon-II.   Good ignite read from here." "SCIEX Juno. IDRIS. Recognized." "Icon-II coming in a bit scratchy Juno. Allow me a few arcs to adjust on XHF….all synched, there. We have zed-100 coming into the Mesosphere. Jachin any climatological readings?" "Negative Proctor. I have no readings…on anything…no data at all on climate or barometric pressure." The IDRIS engineers flew through the Lost Planet's atmospheric layers blindly.

"Back up all updata and link to Juno everyone." Jaxoon commanded the crew. "Juno IDRIS. We have roll plasma thrust and await state vectors." "IDRIS. Juno. Vectors PAD 717.103 Mu. Roll looks good. Stratosphere insertion at 700 arcs PAD at 97 minus 00767 plus 00958 velocity plus 0030 1400 powered descent initiator at plus 70." "Recognized vectors Juno." Seti and the rest of the crew looked out their pod module windows to see if they could make out the surface of the Lost Planet, but the crew could see nothing. The atmosphere around them was glowing iridescent light blue and white.

"Juno we have negative planetary surface data, negative climatological data. Rotational direct is so. We have aft thrusters in 30 arcs. Catarina insert into stratosphere is so. Aft plasma is so." "Recognized IDRIS. Juno confirms aft and stratos insert." "Juno we lost bit rate and uploaded plasma data. PAD 007 we're on dataslip 39-zed." "Recognized Jaxoon. Tetis-Zed and Icon are giving us nothing on surface data or climatological. We expect comm loss in one arc-cycle." "We're as interested as all of you, SCIEX Juno." Jaxoon communicated.

"Ion initialization is so. Plasma residuals at minus 0.1, 0.3, and 0.7 for the tri-thrusters." "Recognized Jaxoon." "Scope is at 70,000 stratos perilune. We should have troposphere insert in 300 arcs. Jachin?" "No data Jadiss. We have nothing. Surface visual should be at Tropos insertion." Jachin the science engineer responded to the module pilot. "IDRIS. SCIEX Juno. Powered descent is so. Initialize aft tri-gimbals. Pitch set 0.9, 0.18, and 0.3. Apogee 47.3. Perilune 9.7." "Recognized Juno. Pitch set 0.9, 0.18, and 0.3. Yew set 000300." "Recognize pitch and yew, IDRIS." The rocket began its powered descent through the Lost Planet's Troposphere onto the surface.

"IDRIS. Juno. Attitude control is good. Pitch 314 yaw 39. Recognize." "Recognized IDRIS. Confirm powered descent. All systems operational." "Tri-gimbal roll is good, we are at 21000 tropos…Juno…stand by….we have a visual on the surface… marginal visual…iridescent mist all over the surface at least at 7000 arci." The crews at the SCIEX Jibiru-Juno control centers hunched together listening to the historic transmissions.

"Throttle down Jadiss. Catarina reading good data here at 11300 arci." Jaxoon informed his pilot. "Still see iridescence on surface mists…no distinguishable geologic formations, or barometric activity." "Recognized IDRIS. Juno has you on manual attitude control. No abstentions to landing. IDRIS you may proceed with landing. We have you at 7000 arci." "Recognized Juno Control. Everything is iridescent up here, we cannot even see Salv. Check that…we have a visual on the surface…strange red haze on the ground…flat level terrain….setting landing coordinates at 119 degrees minus 0.1 from meridian at 3000 arci now." "Recognized IDRIS. Altitude – velocity is median." The rocket's command module began its slow landing onto the surface of the Lost Planet, its thrusters slowing the descent. Seti looked out her pod window at the glowing red landscape and the indigo haze all around them.

"100 arci above surface, landing in 60 arcs." Jaxoon announced to Jibiru-Juno Mission Proctors and his crew. The IDRIS command module landed softly onto the glowing crimson surface of the Lost Planet. "Contact. Full thruster stop. Descent command override off. Extravehicular Environmental Suits activated. EES air flowing." "Recognized IDRIS. We confirm landing." "Juno. Catarina has landed." "Recognized IDRIS! Everyone is exhaling here." "Thank you. Still no climatological or atmospheric data. Terrain is level, flat. From what we can see, thin iridescent haze up to estimate of 3000 arci high. Surface contains red glow emanating about six-and-a-half ars off the surface. Surface appears rocky level terrain." "Recognized IDRIS. You suits should be oxidized and radiated now. Meet us on dataslip 197-zed." "Recognized Juno." Seti and the crew prepared the module for extravehicular activity, and to step onto the Lost Planet for the first time in the history of Opian civilization.

"SCIEX Juno. Module internal pressure is oxidized and recycled. Hatch is open, ladder is deployed, EES fully operational." "Seti has released the Modular Equipment Storage Unit outside Catarina." "SCIEX Jibiru-Juno. EES-3. Comm check." "Recognized EES-3. You have a clear transmission Seti." "Juno. IDRIS EES-1. Comm check and we have video transmission." "Recognized. Comm is clear Jaxoon. Receiving broadcast." "Juno. EES-3. I am at the bottom of the module ladder. The module landing pads are only depressed by a few ars. Surface appears very fined grained, up close….like powder…very translucent…ruddy. I am going to step off the module. Juno Salv takes this step out into the universe together, together in peace." Opians all over Salv huddled before info monitors. Seti's historic words would be remembered by all Opians. In Master Junal's biodome Jaanah and his daughter Juuri, Master Niris, and Junal sat observing the grainy video transmission. Kwai and Tura were not present. "My little Seti-sii…" Junal said as his divis slid around uncontrollably, while his eyes flashed with tears.

"Surface is very powdery but not too coarse. Adheres in fine layers like Febula coal. Gravity is nearly half of back home on Salv. No constraints moving around. Stark majesty as far as I see." "Recognizing, Seti." "Egress from Catarina Juno.

Carbon-dioxide 81 percent. Seti, take my mobile life-support array." "I have it Jaxoon. Guide along the handrails. Come on down!" Seti said to the rocket proctor laughing. If only the Salvs could see them. She look out over the glowing landscape and thought she saw something in the distance. Suddenly, she felt numb, as if her entire skin was vibrating. She tried not to panic, especially now. Her mind began to feel faint, her thoughts could not form properly, as if her consciousness was beginning to shatter.

"Majestic desolation." Jaxoon said as he stepped down onto the Lost Planet. Seti begin walking towards something she could not see, but seemed to be right on top of her. Towering over her. The planet's low gravity allowed her steps to slide longer than they would on Salv's gravity. Jaxoon looked at her confused, and began to feel his body go numb. "Seti, recognize? Uhh.." Jaxoon's attempted to communicate with Seti but his speech slurred. "Repeat Jaxoon…you were breaking up on comm…" "What….those red…my katra…red spheres everywhere…" Jaxoon's transmission was the last communication the Mission Control Proctors on Salv ever received.

The crew inside scrambled to their pod windows to see the cause for loss of transmission, checking on the physical status of Jaxoon and Seti. "All communications offlink! We are at total loss of data! Jaxoon, recognize?" Jadiss shouted, receiving no response from Jaxoon or Seti. All the Opian crew members began shouting at once. "Comm is completely gone. Navigational up, Environmental up, I have no indicators of system-wide losses, where is this coming from?" "No indicators on any networks, Jadiss." Jubilum said. With their space suits oxidized and operating, the crew moved from their pods to the open hatch of the command module. The crew froze in horror at the monolithic spectacle.

Jaxoon walked and half glided towards Seti a few dozen meters ahead of him. His mind exploded, he felt as if his consciousness was hurled from his body into a vacuum of darkness. He couldn't comprehend what happened to him. Somehow, he could see his body striding forward in the space suit towards Seti. He could see Seti standing dozens of meters ahead of him…or below him....where was he? What was he? He could see her….*see* her. Is this death? Jaxoon could not even form a thought, his consciousness was shattered into oblivion, and he was only a spectator to events. The Opian proctor's incorporeal view was all it had. It was a vacuum of complete disembodied madness.

Unaware of the disembodied insanity that "viewed" her from its Void, Seti could see the monolithic landscape before her. She closed her eyes, and tried to pray but could not form intelligible thoughts. Her body went numb, as her consciousness began to shatter into the deeps of the cosmic night. An instant before Seti became disembodied; she looked up to see the monolithic landscape before her. Seti let out a bloodcurdling scream of defiance and disbelief. It was not heard on the Lost Planet.

XV.   JUNO OCCUPATION

"Proctor. Lord Joaz reports no signals or any signs of debris, or combat activity involving the IDRIS in the atmosphere." "Recognized, engineer." Lord Joaz's military Spiden Zed-77 fighter-rockets patrolled the atmosphere for seven cycles after the mysterious last transmission from Jaxoon on the Lost Planet. The Luminist Council announced the loss of the crew to the public, regarding them as heroes. Opians of all tribes, mostly Baali Opians, called for a massive demonstration and march to the twenty-seven biodomes Salvs inhabited.

The Luminist Council and the majority of Opians blamed the Salvs for the loss of the mission. Master Jabulon publicly addressed the Baali Opian tribe, and their leadership triumvirate. Baali Opians numbered forty percent of the Opian population. Jabulon proposed Opians conduct a formal contravention of the first Covenant Gathering between the Lum tribes and the Seven over a thousand conjunctions ago.

The Seven Salv emissaries first approached the Telemesca oracles after the Derobion Wars. Cycles later the Salvs also made conclaves with the High Priest of the Kataan, and the Coridian monks. Since the Covenant, Salvs never interfered with Opian culture, and until the failed landing and previous IDRIS-10 disaster, Opians swore never to involve their space exploration program with the Lost Planet. Jabulon convinced the Baali Triumvirate to contravene the ancient Salv – Opian Covenant.

Kwai and Tura organized thousands of Baali Opians into mass demonstrations and protests against the Luminist Council, which refused to publicly divulge whether Opian legions would take military security actions and prevent Salvs from leaving their twenty-seven inhabited biodomes, or even make any attempts to contact the Salvs at all. The Lums on the Council stated their intentions with the Salvs were under secretive negotiations within the Council. Many Opians grew discontented with the ethnically different Lums that ruled Opian society and the governing Luminist Council. Baali Opians were all Lums, while the majority of Kataan Opians were not the light green-skinned and blue-patterned Lums.

Kwai and Tura sat with Master Jabulon inside his biodome. The two Lums were outraged over the loss of their sister, mourning her at the Council funeral for the IDRIS crew who were all hailed as heroes. Tura mourned the hardest, as he was the younger sibling of Junal's three offspring.

He could still remember being teased by Kwai and Seti at their zooda. Tura's large red eyes flashed as tears fell freely during the stately ceremonies honoring the IDRIS crew. Kwai showed little emotion. He knew Jubilum and Jubila well. Before the mission, his two Baali friends assisted with the organization of demonstrations and infos on the twenty-seven Salv biodomes.

"Tura. Did you authenticate security protocols with Lord Joaz? In case of any activity or aggression from the Salvs, legionnaires will provide secure transport to Jibiru-Juno. " Tura nodded slowly at Kwai. Jibiru-Juno was the Opian Vil where LUMSCIEX Mission Control was located in addition to the Baali confederates operated their Legion Command compound. "I cannot believe this happened. Seti is gone. Jubila. Jubilum. They said to us privately they suspected Salv interference. They believed Seti. In her transferences. They believed the Salvs were using her to trick us. And that she could convince them somehow not to harm the crew." Tura spoke quietly.

"Every alignment the incidents with the Salvs grow more aggressive and dangerous in nature. We were attacked twice by the Salvs, the loss of the IDRIS-10 crew, and now this catastrophe." Kwai's divis twitched angrily as he recalled how he nearly lost his life during the last encounter with the Salv. Somehow, the Salv controlled a Weeping Triphylloid's vine that nearly strangled him, if Tura had not intervened. "You two defended yourself against their psi attacks, even though we have circumstantial evidence the Salvs attacked you two physically, many Opians correlate your accounts of neural distress and attack." Jabulon said to them.

"I have convinced the Triumvirate to halt all Searine production except for exclusive distribution with Baali Vils only." Jabulon said. Baali produced nearly two-thirds of the Searine the Luminist Council agreed to provide for Salvs in a strict exclusive exchange of vital cultural and technological knowledge. "Discontinuing Searine production should have a significant impact on the Salvs. Three alignments ago their Salvs requisitioned a one-third increase in Searine. When the Council compelled Master Serjo to ask for the logic behind the increase the Salvs allegedly stated to him they needed more crystallized vapor for a planned deep space mission. Our sources reveal that the requisition in Searine increase is to compensate for their inability to reproduce and danger of extinction. We believe they need the crystallized red vapor for cloning or to mix with our own genome." Kwai and Tura swayed and slid their divis wildly. Jabulon's explanation was the most logical!

"I will inform the Council we will halt all vaporizing of the Searine flower-crystals effective immediately. I also propose that our confederates introduce formal Council polls that would request Salv emigration onto the Lost Planet or another world they have the technologically capability to reach and relocate. Unless the Salvs vindicate their involvement in curing Rencis and Mnemositis, in addition to their alleged destruction of the Zaxxon satellites and the IDRIS crews. Nine Opians lost their lives at the hands of the Salvs, and Seti!" Tura lowered his head and wrapped his divis slowly around himself hearing Jabulon mention Seti.

"Until the Salvs come forward and offer a precise explanation of their interference in our culture, the Council should request their exodus. And if the Council fails to act on behalf of Opian peace and security, Opian confederated tribes should force the Salvs to relocate." Kwai and Tura knew Jabulon could convince the Baali and majority of the Luminist Council to side with him. The Salvs owed them an account of recent events; the attacks on the Esplanade, the loss of the IDRIS crews, and what exactly was occurring on the Lost Planet.

"Salvs will offer no explanation about the IDRIS disasters. Logic determines that Salvs destroyed the Zaxxon satellites in a preemptive act to prevent communications between Opian legions, making the Lords unable to communicate to each other and the Luminist Council via the S-link." Kwai said. "We would not be able to coordinate with other Legion Lords a unified resistance in the face of any Salv attack." "I am afraid some elements of our own institutions could be involved in the IDRIS disasters." Jabulon flashed his eyes at Tura and Kwai who were shorter than the tall Lum Councilor by half a meter.

Tura and Kwai looked at him curiously. "Who is the only Lum communicating with the Seven? The Emissary of course. The honored Master Serjo, and before him Sothis. Serjo was Kataanese Baali, as was Master Sothis. Nearly all Luminist Emissaries to the Salvs were Kataanese or Coridian. We ascertained that if Salvs wish to control Opian society for their genetic purposes, Kataan and Coridian Opians would be granted stewardship of our race." "I agree Master Jabulon. The Salvic Eye is used in the Luminist banner and Council emblem." Kwai knew the pictograph was used also in popular Opian artistry.

"The Triumvirate has decreed that our Legions engage in defense operations in Misraam and Hira. Misraam Opians have ethnic ties to the Baali including a large percentage of the Hira tribe. Halting all Searine production immediately will force the Kataan tribe to withdraw, and the Council will be driven to allow Baali resettlement of the Elonite and Bahari territories that originally belonged to the Baali." Tura knew his history well and did not disagree with Jabulon, currently one of the most powerful Opians on the Luminist Council. He sought clarification with the Lum Master. "Elonite and the Bahari once were part of the Bahari tribe during the Derobion Wars ay?" Jabulon knew Kwai and Tura had Coridian education in their transzoodas, which would revise historic accounts of the Bahari once were the closest ethnically to the Baali and that the Bahari were sympathetic to the Baali during the Great Derobion Wars.

Master Jabulon called an emergency session of the Luminist Council where he compelled the Lums to poll whether they should formally entreat the Salvs to emigration off the planet. Even though the poll was split by percentage, 48 percent in favor of Salv emigration, and 47 percent against the motion, with 5 percent of the Lums abstaining. According to protocol, the poll could not proceed to formal entreaty or decree. It was still a major popular victory for Jabulon and his Baali Opians. After much fervent shouting and dissent, Jabulon declared the Baali would conduct "strategic operations for the tribal security of the Baali confederacy" in Misraam-Hira territories.

The Baali Opian Master also decreed his tribe would cease all vaporization of the Searine flower-crystals. Master Jodol of the Kataan Opian confederated tribes threatened strategic retaliation with their legions. Within seven cycles, the Baali Opians invaded the Misraam-Hira tribes. The Elonite tribal confederates who received advanced medical and technical knowledge from the Salvs through Emissary Serjo, began air attacks with their Spiden-65 rocket-fighters.

The Elonite Opians defended their Hira allies, while the Bahari Lum Master informed the Luminist Council through his envoy that if Elonite and Kataan Opians attacked Baali territories directly, their legions would provide support to their Baali confederates.

Kwai and Tura organized through Jabulon's info network of communications media Baali tribal leaders and many Searine engineers to gather in the Opian Vil Jibiru-Juno. Tens of thousands of Opians amassed in the Juno side of the twin Baali Vil. Kwai estimated through infolinks that the mass gathering at 39,000 Opians.

Searine engineers, zooda and transzooda proctors, ex-legionnaires, all the crewmembers from the previous manned IDRIS missions, Opians of all social backgrounds joined in the mass assembly. Kwai, Tura, and the crewmembers of previous IDRIS manned missions all addressed the crowd. After three days of speeches and organizing, the crowds swelled to an estimated 70,000 Opians. The masses of Opians began the long march to the twenty-seven biodomes inhabited by the Salvs.

A lone Salv bioship slowly descended over the Lost Planet. Dozens of luminous red orbs carried the bodies of the IDRIS crewmembers, and the Catarina module up into the living bioship. A single red orb descended to the surface and carried Seti's body up to the bioship, flashing red as it hurled up to the waiting bioship. Aboard the ship, Zsiji and Sapia conjoined the ends of their divis to Seti's, beginning the cellular regeneration process that would restore her life. Led by Zsiji and Sapia, the other Salvs on board the ship conjoined their divis, and began melding and morphing; chanting audibly ancient harmonic intonations that echoed through the Hive consciousness. Sapia projected her psionic vital-force all around Seti's body. Salvs melded bodies and morphed into fantastic serpentine shapes, emitting luminous indigo and crimson vapors, punctuated by occasional blue electrical charges.

The harmonic symphony resounded throughout the bioship. Sapia and Zsiji's eyes flashed radiant gold and white. The air around Seti's body grew fluidic and misty as her skin tone returned to its natural green. Time and space seemed to warp inside the bioship as the entire Hive consciousness focused over one hundred thousand years of vital psionic and clairvoyant power on Seti's neural, cellular, and katric regeneration. If Seti's katra could not be restored during the regenerative processes, she would be lost. Incredible psionic and clairvoyant energy surged through Seti's body, emitting indigo vapors and red electric charges. Seti's divis gently wavered, as she opened her eyes.

XVI. THE CAMARILLA COLLUSION

An alignment (a measured period of about three Terran months) had passed since the Juno occupation began. Kwai and Tura organized and led what was now 71,000 Opians marching on foot to the twenty-seven biodomes the Salv species inhabited. During the long march, Opians encountered plants of all colors and shapes, and changing sizes letting out all sorts of wails, cackles, and chortles that assailed their divi senses. Floating Zoyzee, Howling Zephyrids, Glowing Polypoids, gliding Psilocybes, crawling carnivorous Peyotoids, and creatures no Opian have ever seen hovered, swooped, screeched, hobbled, and dashed at them as the Juno occupiers marched to the Salv biodomes.

The first of the crowds arrived outside the central colonnade surrounded by miles of orchards on each side. Between several of the Salv biodomes was a large ornate plaza nearly a mile in each direction. The Salv Great Arcade was decorated with all sorts of planets familiar to Opian biologists, and some they had never seen in the history of their sciences.

The Great Arcade had large colonnades on each side, with towering stone and crystal statues of ancient Salvs, each reaching over a thousand meters high. Living plants, herbs, flowers, and all sorts of sentient phylos native to Salv chirped, chortled, chuckled, and twittered; emitting noises astonishing to Opian divi senses. An indigo mist surrounded the immense plaza.

War broke out between Opian tribes in the alignment since the Juno occupier Opians marched to the Salv biodomes. Baali legions invaded and reoccupied the Misraam and Hira tribal territories. Elonite Opians began massive rocket attacks on the ethnically segregated territories. The Baali tribe in turn attacked the Elonite Opians as their legions occupied their tribal lands within another short alignment. Kataan confederate tribes attacked and invaded the Baali in an attempt to free their Elonite allied tribes. Bahari Opians declared war on the Kataan tribe. With the neutral and peaceful Coridian, Lilim, and Semya tribes into the Baali War.

The Luminist Council was in disarray and turmoil. Several belligerent tribes protested and walked out of the Council amphitheater. Master Jabulon announced he would address the Baali Triumvirate and the Luminist Council in seven cycles. Master Junal invited Jaanah and his daughter Juuri, Ojiri, Niris, Lindra, and Jodol to his biodome so they could safely discuss a peaceful end to the wars that had already killed tens of thousands of Opians. The Opian Lums gathering at Master Junal's biodome all were old friends with him, trusting the old Lum completely.

"We all know of the grave reports coming out of Kataan tribal lands, Master Jodol. Clearly Jabulon and the Baali will not stop the invasions, our intelligence has ascertained the tribal confederates of Semya, and Lilim will be next. Coridian tribes can no longer remain neutral, but we cannot..must not plunge the entire planet into a war." Master Junal said to his friends gathered in his study. "We have not seen such a scale of war and desolation since the Derobion Wars." Master Jodol said, curling his divis sadly. The other Lums slowly curled their divis in agreement.

"We must speak with the Salvs. Recent events and the loss of the IDRIS missions lead them to seclusion. They could have been protecting us from a far greater threat than Opians could imagine on the Lost One." Niris said. "Jabulon's poll agitated the Juno occupation. They will not leave until the Salvs emigrate to another more suitable world. I am afraid the poll has produced grave consequences." Master

Jodol and the other Lums curled and uncurled their divis in solemn agreement with Junal. "Master Seleyis is in seclusion. I fear Jabulon may persuade security force to interrogate him. The Council would force him to contact the Salvs under coercion. Seleyis has been in seclusion under considerable amount of distress since the IDRIS-10 mission." Jodol and the others knew Junal was right. Many Lum Councilors blamed their Emissary for keeping his communications with the Salvs secretive.

Jabulon spoke to the Baali Opian Triumvirate in the Grand Gallery of the Baali capital Vil. Kwai and Tura returned from the Juno occupation at the Salv biodomes back to the Vil by secure transports. The Lum brothers wildly swayed their divis at the historical and political secrets the Triumvirate and Master Jabulon were quietly divulging in front of them and seven other Baali leaders.

"During the era of the ancient Opian Cobolite society, a hidden group of Opians preserved the art, the music, literature, the great sculptures of the Cobols, the Cobol and Uridani Scrolls, the Valtrex Fragments; the Bahari symphonies, the vital essence of our culture for thousands of conjunctions." Kwai and Tura remembered the honored Master Sothis, Serjo's predecessor as Emissary, told them stories of a Lum Camarilla when they were children.

"During the Derobion Wars, the tribes were devastated from millions lost in the fighting. The Kataanese use of chemical vorin gas and the atomic rockets on the Derobion Vils Dhainu and Oreb cost Opians another two million lives. The great Baali, Cobolite, and Lilim tribal confederacies were approached by seven Salvs. The seven claimed they were emissaries of the Salv civilization. Salvs fostered a peace in Opian civilization. Through Lum emissaries that had to undergo several alignments of training,

Salvs systemically providing us with measured increments of their philosophic and technical knowledge. The exchanges occurred over hundreds of conjuctions. They assisted us in the resourceful rebuilding and shaping Opian society after the pestilence and devastation of the Derobion Wars."
"Master Jabulon. Honored potentates. This is basic history taught in first zoodas. Master Sothis used to tell us stories about the Camarilla and the Salvs. How they shaped our civilization after the Derobion wars, and how the Bahari tribe led us to an era of noetic science." Kwai said to the Baali after listening to Jabulon's discourse.

"Opians have always depended on Salvs for technological resources. We agreed never to send probes or crew missions to Lost Planet in exchange for their vital technology. Opians also consented to vaporize Searine flower-crystals for the Salvs." Kwai and Tura were partisan, and Kwai let the Baali know it. "What does this have to do with the Salvs? They have caused the death of ten Opians including Seti! Salvs have caused this war, over their Searine. Salvs want Opian civilization to collapse into tribal anarchic desolation! Then they can make psy-drones out of us, building their bioships that we are forbidden to even set foot on!" Kwai shouted. Jabulon turned and smiled at them.

"Master Sothis, Serjo, and now Seleyis did not include in your stories that the Camarilla are the Bahari. All Emissaries have been Bahari, they are the largest benefactors of Salv philosophic and technical knowledge. The Bahari Camarilla are Lums who have banded together in secret, learning the noetic sciences over the conjunctions. Camarilla Lums have the ability by using the Searine Red Vapor to hide our thought process from the Salvs. Meeting in the temples of the Telemesca and Coridian monks allow the Camarilla to conceal at times our mental process from the Salv Hive." Kwai and Tura's divis twisted excitedly as Jabulon continued.

"The Camarilla are composed of Baali and Bahari, quietly preserving Lum culture through the conjunctions. They are a quiet edifice surviving all empires, conquerors, lords and their tribal wars. We are a comfort to Opians with broken katras, immortalizing the poet, the artist, and musician, the scribe, and wayward Lums consoling the katra silent tragedies. Camarilla are the biography of Opian civilization, and a forging a resistance against Salv control." Kwai and Tura were convinced, attracted by Jabulon's hypnotic discourses.

"The Camarilla has a stratagem? No collusion of this magnitude lasting hundreds of conjunctions would exist without a stratagem." Tura asked. Kwai looked at Tura. He knew the two of them must tell Jabulon and his Camarilla about their deadly encounter with the Salvs and the bizarre scenes they witnessed. "Kwai, they need to know about what we saw." Kwai slowly curled his divis in agreement. "On two separate occasions we encountered Salvs in Master Seleyis' biodome. Seti and Juuri were with them." "Continue." Jabulon said, sliding his divis attentively.

"The vapor was everywhere, surrounding the biodome, and the air was in a misty haze inside. It was not red vapor, the vapors had a bluish indigo haze, like the Febula rings. Kwai and I saw the Salvs changing form, morphing into the most horrifying forms, they were not even bipedal! Seleyis, Juuri, and Seti seemed to be able to separate their katras from the physical body and project them into glowing red spheres. The Salvs also conducted the feat as they melded and shifted. We became physically ill. And...but..." Tura looked down, lashing his divis angrily. "You can tell us Tura." Jabulon comforted. Kwai nodded at his sibling.

"We had a….physical reaction when the Salvs mindshifted with us. A terrible urge to mate, but..the physical pleasure was overwhelming…it was better than mating." Tura admitted. "There is more. Aboard the IDRIS, Jiro and I saw glowing red orbs hurl up from Lost Planet, immobilizing the entire rocket, and destroying the METRIS probe along with the Zaxxon satellites. I theorize this sphere has to do with the katric projections we observed Seleyis and Seti learning from the Salvs." Jabulon and the Camarilla Triumvirate looked at each other in quiet anger.

"Your brave accounts substantiate our hypothesis that the Salvs do inhabit Lost Planet, and possibly have enslaved Opians there. More critically, my friends is that the Camarilla does have a stratagem. Our scientific engineers have reversed the crystallization process, destabilizing the particles within the Searine crystals. That is the Red Vapor. In the event that the Luminist Council fails to act against Salv aggression, we would issue the Nexus Command. Bahari legion-lords can change the command sequence codes of our three atomic rockets. The rockets are auto-sequenced to fire at the Salv biodomes and the Great Arcade." Kwai and Tura looked at each other in surprise at Jabulon's Camarilla stratagem.

"The Juno occupiers are there, they will succeed in forcing the Salvs to emigrate back to Lost Planet or to the horrid corner of the voice they came from." Jabulon smiled at them. "Have the Salvs responded to the Juno occupation?" He asked. "There are no reports of any activity from the Salvs." Tura replied. "Then perhaps we will reoccupy and warrant an explanation from them. We will move the occupation from the biodomes to the Floating Monoliths." Tura and Kwai flashed their eyes in surprise. Salvs forbade Opians to go near the Floating Monolith Pyramids.

Tura and Kwai gathered the other Opian organizers of the Juno occupation to counsel with Jabulon and the Baali Triumvirate. A few cycles later, Kwai, Tura, and the other organizers gave several long orations that were met with resounding support from the tens of thousands of Opians that had established outposts and camps around the perimeters of the Salv biodomes and Great Arcade.

By the thousands the Opian crowd of 78,000 began the long march to the ancient Floating Monolith Pyramids. The ancient site was hundreds of arcos. Opian arcos were the equivalent of a Terran mile. *Now for the first time, Salvs will listen to us.* Tura thought and he and Kwai viewed the tens of thousands of Opians marching to the sacred site.

Many Opian Juno occupiers adorned their garments with the Salvic Eye, a pictograph of a Salv's eye marking with other strange hieroglyphics the exterior of Salv artificial biodomes. The Salvic Eye was also seen by daring Opian scouts on the bottom of one of the Floating Monolith Pyramids. During the Juno occupation and the Baali War, it became a source of Opians identification and scorn with Salvs and their mysterious culture.

Three Salvs sat in meditation inside one of the Salv artificial biodomes. Zevyla, Zephyra, and Zenobia mediated in silence, their advanced minds immersed in the Hive consciousness that had guided Salv civilization across the cosmic expanse. Zenobia, who experienced the first act of violence by an Opian against a Salv in thousands of conjunctions, allowed her clairvoyance to form a voice within the bioweb of the Slav Hive. We cannot survive much longer, we must visit the inevitable continuity of our Katric Camarilla. *The Draags of Ygam share our vital visionary impulses that could regenerate the procreative impulses of Salvs.*

The Hive voiced its collective reply echoing
harmonically throughout the Salv bioweb.
*Transference will be made with the Draags of Ygam.
The Sleep is coming.*

XVII. SETI'S RETURN

Juuri sat with Master Seleyis in his biodome. The old Opian Lum was fragile and still have not fully recovered from the last violent encounter with Tura and Kwai, who interrupted the Salv transference, causing the mindshift to end prematurely. The physical damage Seleyis' old body suffered was worse than the neurological injuries, which the Salvs assisted in regenerating the damaged cells and nerves. "Seti would not tolerate this, she would compel Master Junal and the Council to end this Juno movement." Juuri said. Seleyis understood her revulsion against the occupation. They had believed Jabulon's lies, and sadly he knew Tura and Kwai had also fell victim to Jabulon's hypnotic lies and collusions.

Seleyis could not bring himself to tell Juuri of Tura and Kwai's treachery. Junal lamented to him how he could no longer communicate with his children. He knew Junal really meant he no longer wished to. They had believed in the occupation, tainting their katras with emotional animosity against the Salvs. *They have done so much to help us. Our Katra only knows if they can help save us from ourselves.* Seleyis thought as Juuri frowned, hearing his thoughts within her own mind.

"The Juno occupiers are leaving the biodomes, infos are reporting that they are marching to the Floating Monolith Pyramids." Juuri said to him aloud. "It is forbidden. What will the Salvs do?" Seleyis looked at his old friend's child sadly, slowly twisting his divis around himself. "Salvs will make peace." Juuri was not convinced. "Jabulon has them under his control. They will not listen to the Salvs, or to you Master Seleyis-zan. I fear this will have grave consequences for both Opians and Salvs." Seleyis lowered his head, unwilling to contemplate what she just said. "No….they will not listen."

Juuri gathered her effects and began to exit the study. "They will listen to me. Tura will listen." She said and left the biodome. Master Seleyis slid his divis around his shoulders sadly and returned to reading his infolink. He sighed and put the infolink aside. Baali legions in addition to occupying Misraam and Hira tribal confederacies, also now were systematically routing Elonite legions within their own territories. Baali Opian legions already had entered into Semya Opian tribal territories. *Soon they will come for me. Not before I make a final transference with the Salvs.* Seleyis said to himself, and knew from reading the infolink his lifespan was coming to an end.

Juuri had to use an official Council transport sanctioned by her father, Master Jaanah traveling to the Salv Vil. Departing the Lum transport at the edges of the remote Salv Vil, she made her way to the Salv's Great Arcade near the twenty-seven biodomes. There she encountered nearly one hundred Opians who still remained in the vast colonnades. Juuri approached a Baali tribal advisor she was familiar with, recognizing the female Opian had talked with Tura on several occasions during the Juno occupation.

"Peace to you. I must speak with Kwai and Tura. Do you know their location? It took me three cycles to arrange transport here because of the fighting and the occupation." Juuri said to the Baali advisor. The female Baali looked at her suspiciously. "You are Master Jaanah's daughter ay?" Juuri noticed she did not use the customary greeting between Lums, which she considered insulting. Had Lums lost their own traditions and reverence because the Baali were intent on subjugating as many tribes as they could? Juuri curled her divis apprehensively. "I am Juuri, firstdaughter of Jaanah-zan, Master of the Luminist Convocation." She said formally.

The Baali advisor disdainfully curled her divis, to Juuri it was a clear sign of contempt. "Firstdaughter, how quaint. Tura and Kwai are en route. For security protocols I must ask you to remain with us until your colleagues arrive." Juuri coiled and uncoiled her divis angrily at the Baali woman. "Security protocols? Tura is my mate." *Was my mate*, she thought. "I move freely as I will. If your Triumvirate has matters to resolve with my father, then tell your handlers to make formal polls to the Council, if they are not too busy invading other tribes." Juuri smiled as she spoke.

"Your political affiliations are irrelevant. There are other security matters we need to address relating to the Salvs. I have been advised by Kwai and….your 'mate' to make sure you remain with us." The Baali female's two legionnaire officers moved uncomfortably close to Juuri's at her side. *Of course Kwai and Tura are now mouthpieces for Jabulon's lies* she thought. She moved away from the legionnaires who were already eyeing her suspiciously. "I will remain at the Arcade until Kwai and Tura arrive, but I will not stay with you. I…" Juuri stopped and grew silent suddenly as a Salv emerged from one of the biodomes.

Juuri recognized the spiraling and interlocking indigo patterns on this particular Salv's dark red skin. "ZEB!" She cried out verbally and within her mind. *You are Zeb.* She voiced to the Salv telephatically. The hundred Baali and Bahari Opians in the Arcade saw the Salv and began whispering and murmuring all at once, all of them quickly moving away from the male Salv, giving him a wide berth. The Salv looked at Juuri, hearing her verbally and clairvoyantly. Zeb bowed and undulated his divis ritually at Juuri. Looking at the other Opians still occupying the Great Arcade, Zeb playfully lashed his divis in their direction. Juuri laughed and ran towards Zeb. She did not see the Baali legionnaires and the Baali Lum advisor quickly move behind her, grabbing her they held her firm..

Zeb's large golden eyes flashed, as the three Baali Opians restraining Juuri were knocked ten meters to the ground by an invisible wave. Juuri was not affected by Zeb's telekinetic blast, feeling the powerful invisible psionic blast move through her body. Juuri ran up to Zeb as the Salv taller than her by a dozen meters, knelt down to her level. You are in grave peril precious one. *We must leave our biodomes and this planet.* She heard the Salv's beautiful harmonic clairvoyance echo and sing within her consciousness. She could feel Zeb's voice echo within thousands of harmonic voices within the bioweb of the Salv Hive.

Why? Why must you leave us? Leave our tribes in this state of desolation? Juuri voiced telepathically in reply to the Zeb-Hive. She did not notice the Baali advisor running towards them and the dozen legionnaires running in their direction , crouching in firing positions with their plasma blasters. She did not notice them but she felt them, and could see their actions visualized in her mind.

She could feel Zeb's vast awareness of the Baali, he was aware and the entire horrible scene, had already played out in a causal whirling vortex of time. *We will not leave in our bioships. Salvs can no longer remain on this planet. And we have something wonderful for you.* The Hive voices echoed from Zeb's voice within her own mind. I do not understand …please…help us… but Juuri's transference ended abruptly with Kwai and Tura shouting at her fiercely.

Everything happened at once for Juuri…as if time and space became fluidic and whirling into a vortex of broken reality. "Get away!" She felt and heard Tura shouting as she became disassociated with the entire scene. She felt as if she was arcis above, observing the events with the Salvs. Kwai grabbed Tura before he could reach for Juuri. The legionnaires open fire with their plasma blasters at Zeb striking the Salv in his abdomen and left leg. Zeb hissed in pain audibly as one of blasts also struck Juuri behind her left shoulder. Her shriek was more of disbelief than physical pain, causing her to howl as it soon registered. Clasping her should, Juuri fell to the ground. "Stop firing!" Tura cried.

Zeb's eyes flashed brilliant gold and white, letting out a massive invisible wave that knocked Tura, Kwai, and the dozen Baali legionnaires to the ground seventy meters away. *Into the biodome precious one. Quickly! We will return you to your toola safely.* Juuri heard and felt Zeb's voice sing inside her thoughts. She ran into the vast biodome looked back at the frightened crowd of Opians. Once inside she let out a surprised gasp. The biodome was large enough to inhabit thousands of Salvs. It was a virtual Vil inside, though a Vil could not begin to describe the wonders before her.

Through the indigo vapors inside the central foyer tens of thousands of living phylo plants, Weeping Triphylloids, Glowing Polypoids, Singing Zephytropes, Psilocybes, Red Zootezeems, iridescent blue Daturyte plants gurgled and chortled while towering Red Zootezeems fluttered, cackled and flapped. Myriads of sentient plant life swayed boisterously inside the artificial biodome. Bizarre twisting machines and consoles were somehow fused with organic plants and towering phylo trees. Juuri could hear humming and hissing coming from what she could make out to be massive biomechanical machines in the distance that stretched hundreds of meters high up to the dome.

Salvs had adorned the inside of the dome's covering with vast works of art. Incredible alien paintings of other beings and planets, strange abstract imagery that twisted her mind, stretched across the top of the entire dome's inside. Alien and Salv sculptures fused into various areas of the dome's inside, accentuating the vast paintings. A crawling and hopping beast either she or any Opian biologist ever laid eyes on, hopped up to her and chortled. A long slithering forked tongue lashed out and slid across her hands affectionately, then hopped away on its two webbed legs. Juuri slowly walked forward, astounded. A tiny furry mammal with a long snout and wagging furry tail ran up to her, letting out a strange bark. "woof! woof! woof! The small mammal barked at her and ran away. *This is no biodome.* She thought and said aloud.

You are correct Juuri-sii. This is no biodome. It is a bioship. Salvs inhabit our bioships during deep space travel and when we inhabit this planet or another, the ships undergo a self-transmutation into our biodomes. Zilah and three other Salvs approached her. *It can travel anywhere in the universe and warp into time if we will it.* She heard the Salv Hive echo throughout her thoughts. Now she understood why the Salvs rarely ventured outside their biodome ships. Zilah and the three Salvs guided her into the main passageway where she could see hundreds, perhaps thousands of Salvs engaged in harmonious activity. A few tended to what she could distinguish as consoles within small caverned parts of the dome.

Has…any Opian seen ever set foot inside one of your domes? Her mind was spinning; she could feel thousands of Salvs interacting with her thoughts. Their consciousness interacted with hers fleetingly as if to greet her clairvoyantly. Looking down on of the colonnades through the luminous vapor, she could see bioluminescent indigo and crimson spherical devices spinning with thousands of rings and smaller spheres orbiting around it. Seven Salvs sat around the massive device, their divis attached to smaller orbs connected to strange pod consoles around the titanic sphere. It was one of the most incredible sights she had ever witnessed in her lifespan. *That is the control sphere.* Zilah voiced telepathically.

Outside the biodome, Kwai and Tura rallied the nearly hundred Opians in simultaneously attacking Zeb. Dozens of them threw objects they could loosen and gather from the Arcade. Kwai and Tura retreated to the back of the attacking crowds where the female Baali advisor that spoke to Juuri summoned them to a column of large Baali scientific and legionnaire vehicles. The two Opians recognized the vehicles belonging to Jabulon's elite brigades. Joaz, the Baali legion-lord emerged from one of the vehicles with two Baali soldiers and a group of scientific engineers.

"Kwai. Tura. We have thermally ionized Red Vapor with us." Joaz said. "We have perfected reversing the ionization process for the flower-crystals. Master Jabulon informed you the vapor would be ready for use cycles ago." Tura looked at Kwai. His sibling knew what he was thinking. "Juuri is inside the Salv biodome." Tura said. She is clearly in danger as a hostage, and every Opian remaining here in the Great Arcade is in grave peril." Joaz said. Kwai lashed his divis angrily. 'We will test the vapor. On this Salv." Joaz nodded in agreement with Kwai, and shouted instructions to his brigades and engineers to configure various vapor emission devices in the Grand Arcade.

Zeb fought off dozens of attackers as several more nearly managed to topple him. The Slav received numerous lacerations and bruising from the attacks. It did not take long for Joaz and his brigades to set up and configure twenty-seven emission devices strategically located around the Arcade. "Discharge the vapor!" Joaz shouted. The umbrella-shaped emission devices all hissed in unison as red vapor shot from them in a single red stream towards Zeb.

Zeb's eyes flashed from gold to white in shock as his divi nervous system registered that the vapor was vastly different from the vapor the Salvs used during the meditations and regenerating their bioships. This red vapor was altered and chemically weaponized. Zeb's eyes turned from bright gold to white, his divi nerve system became paralyzed. Stinging with pain, Zeb let out one last invisible telekinetic wave knocking all the one hundred Opians in the Arcade off their feet several meters. Kwai and Tura were hurled into Joaz and against one of the Baali vehicles. The myriads of sentient plant life along the colonnades and orchards surrounding the Great Salv Arcade began to wither and die quickly from the streams of red vapor.

Zeb fell to his knees and collapsed reaching out to Zilah one last time with his consciousness. His last thought was of their mating ritual together. The Salv Hive let out a resounding shriek, echoing throughout the bioweb that genetically linked the consciousness of all Salvs together. Zilah and ten other Salvs rushed from the biodome ship with Juuri quickly following them. Juuri looked at Zeb on the ground, his eyes glazed over white, while his dark red skin slowly faded to a lighter tone.

The ten Salvs behind Zilah slowly picked up Zeb's body and brought it back into the biodome, their eyes also flashing from gold to white as they coughed and retched. Juuri looked at Kwai and Tura, coiling her divis in angry disbelief. She pulled the howling Zilah back with her towards the biodome. Since the Salv was over a dozen meters taller than Juuri, the Opians hands barely reach her abdomen as she gently pulled the Salv along. Zilah softly broke Juuri's slight grasp and stopped in her stride. The Salv looked back at the scattering Opians and at Kwai, Tura, and Joaz in horror.

Inside the biodome, Salvs were mourning Zeb by ritually undulating their divis and chanting a ceremonial soliloquy clairvoyantly. The entire Salv Hive chanted and sung melodically for Zeb. The beautiful symphony resonating within her mind, and every fiber of her katra caused a steady stream of tears from her eyes and divi tentacles. She could hear the harmonic convergence within her mind, thousands of Salv voices singing and all mentioning strange rituals and things she could not comprehend, something about the "Sleep." *Precious Juuri-sii.* The Salv addressed her inside her thoughts.

We have something wonderful for you. We do not mourn precious Zeb. His Katra is now our Katra; it is now NOORI, illuminant, part of every living being in the universe. Juuri did not understand their spiritual conjunction with all living things. Zilah led her down a long colonnade past the central control Sphere. Various living plant life and hovering life forms moved about them, coming from the walls and floors and disappearing into the indigo mist all around them.

Zilah led her into a large cavernous chamber, which had several outcroppings and pods. The outcroppings appeared to be living chambers that could hold at least seven Salvs. As Zilah motion her to approach one of them, a familiar face emerged. Juuri let out a shriek of disbelief as Seti ran towards them embracing her childhood friend.

XVIII.   RED VAPOR

It was chaotic outside the Salv biodomes in the Great Arcade. Master Jabulon communicated to his legion-lord Joaz commanding him in the "order of the ancient Baali Triumvirate and the salvation of the Opian tribes" to detain any Salvs attempting to leave by force, open fire on the biodomes and enter them forcing the Salvs out. Joaz and the other legionnaire officers never questioned Jabulon's orders. He and others after all, were part of a conjunctions-old secret resistance against the Salvs. Jabulon, the Baali, and their Bahari compatriots were the salvation of the Opian tribal confederacies.

Seven cycles after Zeb fell, a Baali team consisting of Joaz, Kwai, Tura, and several Opian rocketeers from previous IDRIS space missions sat in Baali scientific domes in Jibiru-Juno. Jabulon and other scientists were instructing them in the use of the Baali secretly developed psionic weapons. The weapon was a transparent path worn over the left eye. The design of the weapon allowed microscopic nano-sensors to fuse with the ocular cells of an Opian. The ocular nerves were linked to the central nervous system within the divis that connected directly to the brain.

The psi weapon possess microbial Red Vapor in crystallized form that was extremely potent, and could simultaneously act as a receptacle for large amounts of concentrated neuron energy, and a stimulant of neurotransmitters. An Opians alpha wave patterns would be electrically stimulated androtropine levels in the Opian brain, making the Opian hypersensitive to aggression and physical arousal. Androtropine was a hormonal substance found only in Opians.

Wearing the ocular psi-weapon allowed the hyper-aroused and aggressive Opian to reach a state of euphoria. Concentrated violent emotions would active the nanotransmitters in the ocular patch, directing all neuron energy to the patch. By focusing and tapping the patch gently, a neuron electromagnetic wave of energy hurled forward. Kwai sat with his sibling Tura, as the two already were feeling the euphoric effects of the weapon. "The psionic neurotransmitter uses the most dangerous weapon on the planet. The power of our mind." Jabulon said.

"How did this technology come about? How long has the Baali had this weapon, and are other tribes capable of reproducing it?" One of the former IDRIS rocketeers asked Jabulon. Kwai and Tura's divis were lashing about wildly. "Good questions my friend. We perfect the isolation process of the atoms in the Searine crystal only three alignments ago. We reversed the neuron polarity during the crystallization process. Our spies inform us only the Bahari had this technological capability. We could not have achieved this without Bahari engineering." Jabulon explained. "Now we will test the weapon on a Coridian monk accused of subterfuge." Jabulon's guards forcefully dragged a Coridian Opian monk into the spacious test pod.

Kwai, Tura, and the rest of the test team focused their aggressive thoughts against the Salvs and other tribes on the trembling monk before them. As a final act of piety, the monk twisted his divis together forming a circle with them. Tura and Kwai's divis whipped about wildly as they focused on the Opian before them. The rest of the team's patches flashed a brilliant crimson pulsing glow. Kwai and Tura's patches soon replicated the effect as their minds swooned with emotional strain. Suddenly the Coridian Opian flew back into the wall as if an invisible hand hurled him. The Opian fell to the floor, his neck broken.

The next cycle, Jabulon gave a long oration before hundreds of thousands of Opians. He began the spectacle by claiming he would meet with the Luminist Council in private in an effort to stop the war engulfing dozens of Opian tribes. "My Baali tribal kindred, changes of tribal confederacies have occurred frequently in history, and in the history of our people. It is certain, that never was a change of confederacy with such destined results as when the sacred Triumvirate asked me to lead the tribe five conjunctions ago. I was called upon as a custodian of the Great Camarilla at a moment when our confederacy did not seem destined to a great rise. We were given power in circumstances of the greatest conceivable pressure, the pressure of the knowledge that, everything was lost, and that we have been subjects of Salvic will for thousands of conjunctions." Thousands of Opians cheered and held their divis above their heads in solidarity.

"We Baali and Bahari Opians are heirs of a great history. Opians will not know peace until the Salv question has been decidedly disposed of! The Salvs own interplanetary Camarilla has throughout our history usurped the will of the Opian confederacies. No Opian has ever had an aggressive encounter with a Salv until our brave desire to step out into the stars and onto our mysterious neighbor that we believe holds the deepest secrets about our civilizations! Ten Opians were killed in the void of space! Two Opians were attacked within the same period of our brave rocket missions! The Salv have plundered our resources with their Searine requisitions! Salvs have plunged our ancient tribes into war and desolation! The outcome will not be a 'peace' or convention with Salvs; the outcome will be the complete exodus of the Salvs!" Thousands and thousands of more Opians joined in the loud cheering.

"To save our great tribal confederacies from ruin at the will of the Salv, I have ordered Baali and Bahari allied rockets to strike at the heart of their society. Our civilization must flourish free of their control, free from their clairvoyant terror, and control over our brave minds. I have met with Luminist Councilors who hold these revelations as self-evident. Luminist Councilors and my representatives agreed we will permit the Salvs 27 arc-cycles to begin preparations for their exodus from our homeland. Their vast ships can take them to a new world, a better world, where they can live among their own kindred in peace. If the Salv emissaries refuse…if the Salvs remain within their domes, Luminist Councilors and leaders from other tribal confederacies have agreed that our allied legions will begin a great resistance against their Camarilla, and the liberation of all Opians will begin." The Opian crowd grew silent for a few moments, and then erupted in cheers.

The Juno occupiers relocated their massive demonstration and occupation, or "resistance assembly" as they referred to their movement. The Juno occupation dwindled from the original mass assemblies in the Great Arcade at the Salv twenty-seven biodomes. The Juno occupiers now numbered thirty-nine thousand Opians, nearly half the size of the original crowd. The crowd of thirty-nine thousand gathered by surging groups of hundreds and thousands around the Floating Monolith Pyramids. Only a few hundred adventurous Salvs had ever made the long arduous trek to the remote desert region. The site was ancient and sacred to the Salvs. Opians were forbidden to approach the gigantic Floating monoliths, suspended at least one thousand meters in the air.

The Floating Monolith Pyramids were inverted, a luminous crimson and indigo. Tens of thousands of Opians stood several hundred arci away from the inverted Pyramids, suspended incredulously in the air high above them. Night began to fall in the southern hemisphere on Planet Salv, where the Salvs inhabited their biodomes near the planet's warm equator. The planet's Febula rings basked the planet in a violet glow from the outer Febula rings, reflecting the planet's blue star. The inverted Floating Pyramids cast their own mysterious crimson and indigo light down onto the tens of thousands of Opians.

Twenty-seven arc-cycles passed since Jabulon's speech to the Opians at the Vil of Jibiru-Juno. Kwai and Tura returned to the Great Arcade in the Salv biodomes with Legion-lord Joaz, a team of twenty Bahari Opian Lums brandishing the psionic eye patches.

Each of the Lums who had their eye patched with the translucent weapon, including Joaz, Kwai, and Tura, also had the ends of their divis covered with dark red capsules. "The liberation of all Opian tribal confederacies from the Salvs has begun." Kwai said to Tura and the other Opian psi-regiment.

Tura and another regiment moved the Red Vapor emission devices from their legionnaire vehicles into small mobile pods around the perimeter of the colonnades. "Juuri is still in that biodome." Kwai said to Tura, pointing at one of the twenty-seven Salv biodomes Juuri fled into cycles ago when Zeb fell. "She is mine." Tura replied flashing his large red eyes, and lashing his divis about feverishly. A thousand Juno occupiers quickly retreated away from the Baali and Bahari legionnaires, observing the operations, cheering loudly and brandishing benta shafts. Kwai heard the familiar unmistakable whine of legion rocket-fighters approaching the Salv biodomes. "Here the they come." He hissed.

The Opian technologically advanced Spiden-77 rocket-fighters could out maneuver and outgunned any class of Opian rocket-fighter in all the tribal legions combined. Two dozen Spiden rocket-fighters circled the vast perimeter of the twenty-seven biodomes. With several snap-hisses, the rocket-fighters fired their ion and plasma rockets at each of the Salv biodomes. Most of the rockets exploded in brilliant flashes of white, vaporizing by an invisible force within the indigo mists that surrounded the biodomes. A few of the rockets landed in the colonnades and sprawling orchards surrounding the biodomes, setting them ablaze.

The rocket-fighter pilots relayed back to Legion-lord Joaz that the plasma and ion rockets were ineffective against the biodomes. "Execute command Juno Zero." Joaz communicated with the lead rocket pilot from one of the command pods established in the Great Arcade. "Recognized." The lead pilot replied. The pilots in the two dozen Spiden fighters switched on an engine configuration panel inside their flight pods, as they swooped high away into formation. The Spiden fighters engines flashed a let out a quick loud burst. The rocket plasma glow faded and red gaseous vapor streamed out from the engines as the rockets each dove two by two into the Salv biodomes.

The crowd of Juno occupiers gasped and shouted loudly as red streams with rockets at the end entered into a controlled dive towards the biodomes. Each of the two rocket-fighters crashed into the Salv habitats erupting in large balls of blue and orange plasma explosions. Streams of red vapor lingered downward from the suicidal flight paths. Twenty-three of the biodomes blazed with plasma fire, the thick black smoke rising above them and the Opians in the Great Arcade. Several of the biodomes had their structural exterior breeched with gaping fiery holes large enough for Opians to penetrate and enter.

Opians glimpsed at the massive organic and biomechanically engineered pathways inside the domes, the vast translucent control pods, and their flashing consoles, strange arrays of fantastic towering sentient plant life. All chaos broke loose inside each of the biodome ships as Salvs ran and glided back and forth attempting to repair the damage areas. "Discharge the Red Vapor." Joaz communicated on his infolink with the legionnaires in the Great Arcade. The mobile emission pods shot streams of red vapor all around the biodomes and Great Arcade. Dozens of Opians carried the mobile emission pods to the entrances of the burning biodomes. The Red Vapor discharges could be seen for thousands of miles by Opians, whose biological makeup prevented the toxic fumes from having fatal effects.

Hundreds of Opians choked and hyperventilated from the streaming vapors surrounding the biodomes and Arcade. The Red Vapor's toxic fog crept slowly into the Salv biodomes, causing thousands of Salvs to retch and choke, their eyes flaring horrid white flashes, a deadly distinction from their large captivating golden lidless eyes. Within an arc-cycle, the choking Salvs fell lifeless, unable to begin the complex cellular regenerative process that would heal cell membrane, nerves, and any other physical trauma.

Inside the biodome where Zilah had led Juuri to reunited with Seti, the two Opian Lums clasped each other in terror as the rocket-fighters plunged into their biodome. Cycles before the attacks, Seti rushed to embrace her childhood toola-friend. Seti recounted how the Salvs regenerated her body, saving her life and placed her safely aboard their bioship where it took her several alignments to rehabilitate completely from the trauma of the IDRIS-11 expedition. With Zsiji, Sapia, and dozens of other Salvs sitting around them, Seti slowly revealed to Juuri what happened, and what she witnessed on the doomed expedition to the Lost Planet.

Juuri's eyes flashed white and her divis straightened in shock.

Now as the Red Vapor began to fill the biodomes, Zenobia telepathically voiced inside Seti and Juuri's thoughts. *Precious ones…the time of the Sleep has come. You must return to your toolas. You will be safe. Savene will accompany you to your toolas. You must go now.* Juuri and Seti clasped each other trembling as they saw thousands of choking and retching Salvs falling onto the ground inside the biodome ships, many of the struggling to get back up, most of them falling lifeless, their golden eyes flashing to a pale white. *What is happening!* Seti and Juuri both cried in clairvoyant unison. *We will meet again. Take your toolas to the Floating Pyramids and await us there. You will be safe. This will be our final communication with you. Please recite this message to as many Opians and toolas as you can exactly as we dictate… The Lost Planet is….*

Savene, a slender Salv with brilliant interlocking violet patterns on her dark red and indigo skin, walked with Juuri and Seti to the main foyer of their biodome, the red vaporous fog dissipating the glowing indigo mist inside. Several hundreds of Salvs began walking slowly out of the burning biodomes and red fog surrounding them. Kwai and Tura tapped their psionic eye patches to no effect. Hundreds of Salvs continued to walk out of the burning and foggy biodomes slowly. Their recognizable silhouettes walked in a ghostly manner to the Arcade. Tura looked into one of the gaping holes in the biodomes where part of the structure collapsed. He shrieked in shock as he saw Juuri and an Opian who looked like Seti.

Tura found Kwai amidst the clamor and smoke pointing and yelling at the gaping burning entrance to a biodome. "It's her. It's Seti!" Kwai looked and shouted in disbelief. Seti was alive, either alive or a clone or some sort of Salv experiment. The two ran towards the biodome and saw a Salv guarding Juuri and Seti. "Seti! Seti!" Kwai screamed and choked in the red vapor. Tura coiled his divis tightly and clenched his teeth letting out a feral growl. He tapped his eye patch yet to his dismay, the patch had no effect on the Salv. Juuri and Seti saw Kwai, Tura and several dozen legionnaires running towards them fast. The two Lums fled back into the burning biodome. Savene stood in the main foyer as an entire section of the burning dome collapsed on them.

Kwai and Tura howled in pain as their flesh seared with burning pain. "Salv…please…help us …you're all in danger…the nexus comm…Salvs…" Kwai's voiced trailed off and grew quiet as his eyes flashed white staring into the eyes of the female Salv who lay next to him. "Salv…keep them safe …. please…" Tura's last thought was not of Juuri, nor was his last thought his own. His last conscious awareness was of the harmonic and beautiful Salv voice within his mind. *My Katra is now your Katra precious illuminant. We will join with Noori in peace. Rest now precious one.* Tura's eyes flashed white as his mind finally quieted forever.

Seti and Juuri ran into Zsiji and Sapia who were walking with hundreds of other Salvs out of the foggy red burning biodome ship. Zenobia moved to their side and motioned to the two Opian Lums to follow her, and quickly. Hundreds of ghostly Salv silhouettes moved slowly about the Great Arcade and suddenly arched their divis. A massive telekinetic wave hurled all the Juno occupiers and Opian legions off their feet to the ground, thirty meters away, knocking them unconscious. Thousands of Opian bodies lay strewn about the Great Arcade, unconscious but breathing.

In outer space, hundreds of Opian satellites lost power and hurled from orbit, into the planet's Febula Rings. The hundreds of Opian satellites burned up in the Salv atmosphere, putting on a grand display of raining streams of light, resembling shooting stars. All across Salv, several major Opian Vils systematically began losing their power grids.

At the Floating Pyramids, the crowds clamored raucously as news of the events at the Salv biodomes and Arcade reached their infolinks. Suddenly the air around and beneath the suspended monolithic Pyramids began to fluctuate into a fluidic transparency. The inverted Pyramids seemed to vibrate slightly into the fluidic transparency surrounding them. Tens of thousands of the Juno occupation Opians were knocked forcefully to the ground, unconscious. Nearly forty thousand Opians lay strewn about, breathing and cataleptic. Above them, the inverted Pyramids remained suspended and silent; their indigo and crimson glow cast a shadow over the unconscious Opians.

XIX. SALVS AND DRAAGS

Millions of Light years from the ringed Indigo cosmic jewel that was Planet Salv, the Draags of Planet Ygam were conducting massive de-omisations. The Oms were reproducing at appalling rates, and showed signs of intelligent thought as several Draags had discovered vast organized settlements of untamed, wild Oms. On Ygam, a long-awaited day arrived for an entire generation of Draag adolescent children. Their first meditation was a critical initiation ceremony that marked an essential step on their road to intellectual maturity. Red meditation spheres hovered slowly above the Draag Uvas, containing ethereal projections of their vital essence.

Tiva sat meditating inside the Draag ceremonial initiation chambers. Her essence formed inside the glowing red spheres and hovered high above her Uva. Tiva's intimacy with her pet Om, Terr, waned as she matured and learned the ancient rituals of Draag meditation. When Terr could no longer benefit from the vital philosophic knowledge from Tiva's infos, he ran away with her info headset. Terr's adventures with the wild Oms away from Tiva would unknowingly affect the course of four civilizations.

Tiva's father, Master Sinh, sat in transcendent meditation with the other Draag Prime Ministers. Master Taj, Master Kon, and two other Draag Prime Minister sat with Sinh in the fantastic melding meditation. The Draags began the strange ritual, by transcending their thought process and vital essences. Such a discipline approach to meditation and their neural impulses allowed the meditating Draags to morph their physical bodies into fantastic and bizarre abstract shapes. The iridescent melding Draags morphed their physical bodies repeatedly, with transcendent intellectual and philosophic revelations occurring with their collective consciousness with each colorful melding. Their physical forms shifted, morphing into abstract shapes, their consciousness shifted in transference with other beings millions of light years away, yielding chimerical visions.

Master Sinh and the other Draag Ministers did not see young Tiva peeking into the chamber from behind a vaporizer unit. Since the initiation ritual of her critical first meditation, Tiva's interest in the sacred ritual had grown with her intellectual maturity. When Sinh and the other Ministers concluded the melding meditation, Tiva ran back into her chambers. Sinh and the other Draags returned their transcendent consciousness to their physical bodies. Master Sinh interrupted the silent respite. "Our chimerical meditations were vital this time. We must go to the Fantastic Planet, and await the Salvs."

Tiva completed a cycle of her infos. "Tiva. Have you found your Om?" "No father." She replied softly. "Terr is gone. Mother and I could not return him with the bracelet." " I fear this may have unintended consequences." Master Sinh said. "Father. I want to join with the meditations on the Fantastic Planet." Tiva said. "No Tiva. When you are ready, you may join us. You must first learn the melding meditation rituals." "Yes father." Tiva thought of Terr on occasion. Her interest in Oms waned as her intellect matured rapidly for a Draag. Tiva was determined to learn the transcendent Draag meditations.

Luminous red meditation spheres floated and drifted high above the Uvas of Ygam. The Draags projected themselves into the radiant spheres, hovering through the Draag atmosphere toward the Fantastic Planet. Thousands of luminescent pulsing spheres glided onto monolithic white humanoid statues on the Fantastic Planet. The statues were titanic hybrid biological-machines, controlled by the consciousness of the beings that fused with them. The red meditation spheres hovered atop the headless statues and awaited the Salvs.

Luminescent indigo and red meditation spheres of the Salvs arrived shortly after the Draags. Draag and Salv meditation spheres each hovered and descended atop the headless hybrid statues. Joining in ritual nuptial meditations, the Draags and Salvs animated the monolithic statutes with the vital life-force. The animated statues danced ritually, engaging in strange concupiscent intercourse by means of the animated statues controlled by their meditation spheres. During the nuptial rituals, Salvs and Draags communed via consciousness transference within their meditation spheres. Draag and Salv conducted their chimerical melding meditations inside the spheres allowing them to commune with one another.

They extracted from these strange nuptial rites, the vital visionary impulses that made procreation possible. This ensured the perpetuation of both the Salv and Draag species. The bioweb of the Salv Hive consciousness communed with the melding Draags. *Your race shares our vital visionary impulses that could regenerate the procreative impulses of Salvs. Our race is in peril precious ones. We can no longer procreate. Our unsustaining cohabitants of Salv have grown aggressive and seek to destroy our species.* The Draag Council in the mind transference contemplated their dilemma with the Oms.

Draags face a similar conundrum with a domesticated species that reproduces at appalling rates, and may have once been a technologically advanced civilization. Our scientists believe these Oms from the ancient planet of Terra may have destroyed their entire civilization. Draags and Salvs must ensure the regeneration of both our species. The Salv Hive responded to the clairvoyance voices of the Draags. *One day Opians may enter our fellowship. Perhaps the Oms you speak of may also join in our fellowship. When they reach an imaginative development of noetic sciences.* The Draags contemplated the strange possibility suggested by the Salvs. *Oms are unsustainable, and if our scientists our correct their predictive evolutionary patterns could relapse into self-destruction. The vital evolutionary impulses of Salvs are far more advanced than any being we have encountered here on this Sanctuary.*

The Salv Hive echoed within the Draag mind transference. *Many species like the Oms and Opians throughout the first generation galaxies may surprise our civilizations one day. Our evolutionary vitality originates in the inevitable continuity of Katra; our intellectual histories and visionary impulses stored collectively in lattices of our genetic code. Katra is our visionary will that seeks to live and die, originating from Prime Reality, what our race calls the NOORI, the sole existence that binds all life forms together.* The Draags learned from the vital philosophic knowledge of the Draags as the melding meditations drew the nuptial rights to a climax.

Draags share a similar philosophy with the Salvs. We call your lattices of Prime Reality 'Ames.' Our philosophic knowledge teaches us the Great Zarek hurls forth from the Prime Reality in the flames of time into whirling realities, multiplying infinitely combating the Draag Ame, which seeks to die. The Draag 'Ame,' we believe is compatible with the Salv Katra. These principles form the basis of our meditations. The Salv Hive replied as the strange nuptial rites animated by the undulating and dancing monolithic statues climaxed.

Prime Reality, the Noori, is a reflection of the visionary essence of all life. Katras, similar to the Draag Ames, resemble lattices of light, like brilliant stars enclosed in crystals that are the various life forms across the universe. Our meditations will ensure the regenerative perpetuation of our species. We will sleep for a long time and awaken to meld again with Draags on this planet. The bizarre nuptial rite reached its climax as the Draags departed the Fantastic Planet in their meditation spheres. The Salvs departed the desolate planet in their luminous indigo and red meditation spheres.

XX. OPIAN CONVERGENCE

Planet Salv hung in the cosmic expanse illuminated as an indigo jewel in space. The planet's Febula Rings reflected the light of its blue star into the atmosphere, casting a luminous indigo glow all around the darkened planet. Many of the Opian Vils had lost all their power grids. Simultaneously, hundreds of Opian satellites lost their power and fell from orbit, raining into the Salv skies as they burned up in the atmosphere, resembling myriads of shooting stars.

Nearly a thousand Opians lay strewn about, cataleptic around the foggy Great Arcade of the Salv biodomes. The air was still a red haze from the emission weapons of the Opian's Red Vapor. Several thousands of Salvs lay choking and gasping for breath inside their biodomes.

The bodies of Kwai and Tura lay lifeless beneath a partially collapsed Salv biodome. Savene lay next to them, her lifeless eyes pale white. At the Floating Monolith Pyramids, forty thousand Opians participating in what they called the Juno occupation also lay catatonic.

Jabulon, several Opian legion-lords, and their sub-commanders were in a dimly lit Jibiru-Juno LUMSCIEX Control Center. The Control Center operated on minimal reserve power from mobile pod generators. Various legionnaires were shouting, as the entire Center was chaotic. "The Salvs will destroy us! The Camarilla is moving to take control of all our resources. Our satellites are all destroyed we have no communications!" One of the legion-lords shouted at Jabulon. Several other allied Luminist Councilors gathered inside the main control chamber with Jabulon and his subordinates.

A Bahari Opian spoke up, quieting the other Councilors. "Masters. Never has our civilization faced such peril! We must issue the Nexus Command!" Master Jubilo said. "The Nexus Command can only be issued by unanimous consensus of the Luminist Council!" One of the other Councilors protested. "Masters, Jubilo is right. For all we know, a Salv legion could be massing to assume control of our Vils, and enslave us." Another Lum Councilor said. Jabulon spoke up at last. "The Luminist Council is no more. The Salvs have been in control of the Luminist Convocation for over a thousand conjunctions. The Councilors that are not part of our resistance against the Salvs are part of their Camarilla." The other Councilors agreed, lashing their divis wildly.

"Long before Sothis Salv control of our civilization was set in motion. The Salv stratagem has come to culmination under Serjo and now Seleyis and his elitist Camarilla have brought us to ruin and enslavement at the hands of Salvs!" Jabulon shouted raising his divis high above his head. "Master Jabulon. If we poll the Nexus Command the Baali Lums must stop the fighting!" Jubilo said. "Our legions will cease hostilities in all tribal confederacies once the Nexus Command is given. You have my word Masters." "If we issue the Nexus Command we will not have a civilization to save!" A Lum Councilor said. Jubilo looked at him scornfully. "If we do not issue the Nexus Command, there will not be an Opian civilization! " Jubilo shouted.

"I will not condone the Nexus Command. Masters will poll." Jabulon instructed. The seventeen Luminist Councilors each polled for authority to issue the command that would launch an atomic strike on the Salvs. One of the last Councilors polled refused to give consent. Jubilo motioned for a legionnaire to hand him his plasma blaster. The dissenting Lum stepped back and raised his arms in shock as Jubilo fired three times into his chest. Jubilo handed the weapon back to the soldier. The other legionnaires in the control chamber raised their plasma blasters ever so slightly implying there would be no further dissent. "The poll is unanimous." Jubilo said Jabulon and the other fifteen Lums.

Jabulon nodded at his Bahari ally. Jubilo and Jabulon walked to a secluded section of the Command complex, followed by the fifteen Luminist Councilors and half a dozen legionnaires. The entire Control complex was dimly lit with reserve pod generators only providing power for critical areas of the large domed building. Jabulon and Jubilo approached a large double wooden door, and inserted their dataslips into the doors console. They entered a large dual layered chamber with seven legionnaires inside operating three circular consoles.

"Initiate the Nexus Command sequence. By authority of the Luminist Convocation and of the great tribal confederacies." Jabulon said and handed his dataslip to three legionnaires hunched over one of the circular consoles. The other four Lum technicians hesitated before slowly taking out their dataslips. Each of the seven launch technicians inserted their dataslips in sequence one after another.

After the dataslips were inserted into panels on the control consoles, each of the seven technicians inserted small keys into the panels and pressed sequences of buttons on their console. The engineers hesitated and turned to Jabulon one last time. Jabulon nodded at them. "Begin the sequence now." Jubilo said as the seven engineers turned their firing keys sequentially.

Thousands of arcos away in the vast Salvic deserts, three rockets blasted into the skies from hidden launch pads. The atomic rockets soared towards the

Salv Vil where their twenty-seven biodomes were located. In the Jibiru-Juno LUMSCIEX Control Center, Master Jabulon turned to Jubilo. "The Nexus Command includes contingencies other than the rockets. Master Seleyis and the remaining Councilors at the Great Amphitheater must be detained and interrogated until we can ascertain the extent of their collaboration with the Salvs. There are reports that Salvs rescued Seti on the Lost Planet after the failed IDRIS-11 mission and she has been living among the Salvs. If she is located she must also be detained and brought before our tribunal." Jabulon said. "Jubilo and I will take three brigades with us to the Great Amphitheatre." "Masters. Twenty arcias until the rockets reach the target."

Thousands of Salvs lay lifeless on within the smoldering biodomes. The bioweb was beginning to fragment. The Salv Hive was unable to begin the cellular regenerative process or converge enough psionic energy to restore their Katra. Hundreds of Salvs were walking about among the catatonic Opians outside their biodomes. The ghostly silhouettes of the Salv moved about the Great Arcade by the hundreds. Inside one of the biodomes, the last of the fallen Seven Emissaries sat in meditation. Zevyla, Zilah, Zsiji, Zenobia, and Zephyra formed glowing indigo and red meditation spheres around their bodies protectively.

The time has come precious ones. We must go to the Floating Pyramids now. The Salv's bioweb was straining inside the Hive consciousness. For the first since the ancient Rite of Salvis Psychotria, the Salvs began to feel emotional impulses. Thousands of Salv harmonic voices rang out in unison to the Hive consciousness. Never had the Salvs felt their collective consciousness so fractured.

Peril approaches. We may not have enough time to stop the impact. Sapia and Zsiji voiced in unison to the Hive. *We can de-ionize the polarity of the weapons. Now precious ones.* The Salv Hive converge their entire psionic vital essence on the three approaching atomic rockets. They could not alter the course of the rockets without radioactive effects to the Opians. Sapia suddenly had an idea. . Zevyla, Zilah, Zsiji, Zenobia, and Zephyra all concentrated. The red meditation spheres flash a luminous red. *Reverse the polarity of the neutron flow.* Sapia voiced.

The atomic rockets blasted into the Salv biodomes without detonating. The impact of the rockets still caused the complete collapse of one of the biodomes. *We cannot remain. The effect of the red vapor will become irreversible. We must commune with the Draags before the Sleep.* The Hive Consciousness could only sense the vital life-force of a few hundred living Salvs. *The Hive is breached. We will begin the regenerative process inside the Floating Pyramids.*

A mobile electric generator pod provided marginal power in Master Junal's biodome. Zenobia a former emissary of the Seven sat with a joyfully reunited Seti and her father. "They brought you back to me precious one. Just like they brought Juuri-sii back to Jaanah-zan." The remaining members of the Luminist Council gathered into the Great Amphitheater along with Junal and Seti. Seti was given a seat at the rostrum with the other Councilors. Master Junal assisted Seleyis to the rostrum. Ojiri, Jaanah, Niris, Lindra, and Jodol were the only other living members of the Luminist Council.

Jodol spoke first after the ritual opening of the Council. "The Baali stopped the fighting but Jabulon and his security brigades are still fighting the Hira and Semya tribes." "The fighting is over. The people are scared Masters. How do we know the Salv's intentions are peaceful?" Ojiri and Lindra nodded and coiled their divis in agreement, listening to Jodol. "Tens of thousands of Opians are catatonic! Vils are systematically losing power! All our satellites appeared to have lost their orbits and burned up in the atmosphere! Baali legions are still terrorizing tribal confederacies! Do the Salvs want to destroy us?" Ojiri cried. The other Councilors began shouting at once.

Suddenly the Councilors heard a large explosion followed by several dozens of Opians running toward them in the Council Hall of Convocation. Two dozen legionnaires burst open the doors into the dimly lit rotunda with plasma blasters raised. Jabulon and Jubilo strode in behind them. "So the stories are true. Seti you not sit at the Luminist rostrum after living among your Salvi mates?" Jubilo scoffed. Jabulon motioned for the legionnaires to grab Seleyis.

"This is how the Luminist Council now conducts our affairs Jabulon? With plasma blasters?" Junal asked. The guards struck Seleyis hard, knocking him to the floor unconscious. The other Councilors gasped as Seti rose. Her large red eyes flashed a brilliant gold, sending a wave of telekinetic force that hurled Jubilo, Jabulon, and the other Opian soldiers across the room. Jabulon's soldiers were knocked unconscious. Jubilo helped him back to his feet as the two Lums grabbed plasma blasters from the unconscious soldiers and aimed at Seti.

Juuri stepped out from behind the corner of the rostrum and fired her own plasma blaster at Jabulon and Jubilo. Her plasma bolts struck Jubilo and Jabulon in their divis. The two Opians shrieked in pain and fell to the floor disoriented. "Are you all right Juuri?" Her father Master Jaanah asked as Luminist guards entered and began detaining the now semi-conscious conspirators. "Yes father." Juuri said. "Jabulon, Jubilo, and any Opian who brought harm to a Salv will stand before a tribunal." Master Junal declared.

"Father. Masters. We must go to the Floating Pyramid Monoliths. The Salvs will await us there." Seti said quietly. The course of Opian civilization was about to change. "The Salvs instructed me to repeat a message. And we must all listen and go to the Floating Pyramids." Lum homeopaths were tending to Seleyis grimly as they carried him away. "The journey to the plateau will take several cycles Seti." Jaanah said. "What do the Salvs voice to Opians?" Seti smiled and turned to the Lums. *The Lost Planet is… …"*

XXI.   FANTASTIC PLANET CONJUNCTION

Luminous indigo and red meditation spheres hovered above giant white iridescent hybrid statues. Hundreds of Salvs sat in melding meditation inside the glowing orbs awaiting the arrival of the Draags. On planet Ygam, the home of the Draags and their tiny human pets, the Oms, radiant red meditation spheres floated and drifted into the skies of Ygam. The glowing red spheres contained the vital life essence of the Draags.

Tiva's Om, which she named Terr after she found him as a babe, had escaped with her info headset, and encountered wild Oms living in the savage wilderness of Ygam. Terr introduced the vital technological and philosophic knowledge of the Draags to several untamed Om tribes, using Tiva's info headset. The human Oms began to rebel against their Draag masters, becoming increasingly capable of reproducing Draag technology.

Walking along a colonnade, two Draag adults discovered a wild Om settlement, and attempted to stamp it out. The tiny human Oms attacked one of the large blue-skinned Draags, pulling it to the ground and killing it. This act of violence startled the Draag Council into conducting massive de-Omisations. De-Omisations wiped out entire settlements of human Oms using advanced Draag weapons.

The Oms ability to reproduce Draag technological marvels grew exponentially. Fearing more massive de-omisations, a now adult Terr lead several tribes of Oms to an abandoned Draag rocket depot. Oms constructed a city there over time as one Draag season equaled a span of fifteen human years. The remaining domesticated and wild Oms joined Terra in the Om city. The Oms built two rockets, designed to take them to Ygam's natural satellite.

The Draag Council coordinated a massive campaign of de-omisation across the entire planet. The Council even questioned whether they should keep their domesticated Oms. As the massive de-omisation threatened to purge the Oms living in the rocket depot city, Terr decided they must launch their rockets in hopes of moving the remnants of their civilization away from the Draags.

Two Om rockets blasted off from the abandoned Draag rocket depot. The rockets hurled through the atmosphere of Ygam towards its natural satellite. Terr and the Oms on the rockets were unaware of the hundreds of drifting red mediation spheres around them as the rockets soared past the glowing spheres. Within the span of Terran day, the Om rockets landed on Ygam's natural satellite, which the Draags called the Fantastic Planet.

The Oms marched out of the rockets by the hundreds, amazed that the air was breathable. The Draag meditation spheres drifted above the skies with the Salv spheres. Inadvertently, the Oms led by Terr had discovered the secret of the Fantastic Planet. The wayward human Oms gazed up at thousands of towering white headless humanoid statues. The statues were monolithic hybrid bio-machines, controlled by the consciousness of the beings that fused with them in the meditation spheres. The glowing spheres descended atop the hybrid organic-automata where a head normally would sit atop the huge humanoid.

The monolithic biological-automata terrorized the tiny Oms who ran back to the apparent safety of the rockets. Conjoining in strange nuptial rites, the Draags and Salvs animated the huge bio-automata statues with their vital life-force. The Draags called it, *Ame*, and the Salvs called their vital intellectual and spiritual essence,

Katra. The animated hybrid beings danced ritually, engaging in strange intercourse through the animated statues controlled by meditation spheres. The communing Draags and Salvs danced all over the Fantastic Planet, engaging in intercourse via melding meditations. They extracted from these fantastic nuptial rites, the vital visionary impulses that made procreation possible again. This ensured the critical regeneration of both the Salv and Draag species.

The bizarre dancing and alien nuptials terrorized the Oms, as the hybrids were moving to close to the rockets. The enormous feet of the giant statues threatened to smash the Om rockets. "We must do something Terr!" Terr had to act fast to save the human Oms. "Yes. Activate the disintegration ray." The rockets fired disintegration beams developed from advanced Draag technology at the dancing automata statues. The statues crumbled into pieces, breaking apart. The luminous red spheres of the Draags floated wildly about with the indigo and crimson Salv meditation spheres. Interrupting the nuptial intercourse caused a chaotic chain reaction.

Chaos engulfed the Draag civilization on their homeworld. Salv meditation spheres drifted and floated adrift aimlessly. *What has happened?* The Salvs telephatically communicated with the frantic Draags inside their spheres. *It is the Oms. They have fired upon us!* The Draags voiced clairvoyantly to the Salv Hive consciousness. *The Oms from the planet Terra. You must find a way to live in conjunction with them, as we live in conjunction with the Opians.* The Salvs responded. *We will find a way to conjunction. Our procreative impulses will not be affected from this catastrophe.* The Draags voiced and returned to planet Ygam.

"Never have the Draags been faced with such imminent disaster!" One of the Draag ministers cried out. "Our entire civilization is doomed!" Another lamented. "The Oms have taken revenge!" "They have incredible technical knowledge at their disposal!" "How could they evolve so rapidly?" "We must destroy them!" The Draags all shouted at once. "Yes, but how? How?" "The de-omisations have failed its already too late!" Master Sinh thought of his chimerical mediations on Fantastic Planet with the Salvs and the procreative enterprise they shared. "There is only one solution. Neither the Oms or the Draags want to destroy themselves. We must somehow make peace."

Terr and the rest of the human Om representatives agreed to go to the Draag Council and make peace with their former Masters. Master Sinh was astonished to see Terr leading the Oms. "That was Tiva's Om!" He exclaimed. Draags and Oms agreed to a conjunction. No Om would ever return to the Fantastic Planet. The Draags abandoned their campaigns of de-omisation and domestication of free human Oms.

It had been a generation since the Era of Sinh, the period of the Masters of Ygam. Significant evolutionary changes occurred in the civilizations of the Draags and Oms. The Draags granted Oms systematic access to the Draags vital philosophic and technical knowledge. In exchange, the Oms instilled their vitality and resourceful work habits into the imaginative thought cycles of the Draags.

Tiva, now a fully matured adult Draag, hypothesized about her role in fostering peace between the Oms and Draags. Some Draags believed the Great Zarek, emerging from the flames of time into whirling reality compelled the Draags to shift into critical evolutionary changes. Tiva hypothesized the remarkable changes in the imaginative evolutionary impulses of the Draags were caused from their nuptial rites with beings form other galaxies on the Fantastic Planet. When the relocation of nearly all Oms to their artificially constructed satellite came, Terr had lived out his human lifespan as Tiva matured into an adult Draag.

Tiva and her compatriot's chimerical melding meditations were vivid. The long awaited day arrived when Tiva and the other Draag Prime Ministers would undergo their first nuptial rite on the Fantastic Planet with the Salvs. The strange chimerical alien conjunction occurring on the Fantastic Planet with the Salvs would change the course of fate for the First Generation Galaxies.

Night was somnolent blue on the Fantastic Planet...a single iridescent red mediation sphere arose and hovered...

XXII.   FLOATING MONOLITH PYRAMIDS

Hundreds of Salvs slowly walked from the ruins of their smoldering biodomes to the ancient site of the Floating Monolith Pyramids. Opians from all over the planet gathered to watch. Over a million Opians and Lums converged on the ancient plateau sacred to all Salvs. Many of the Opians and Lums trekked to the Floating Pyramids out of curiosity, many simply to display their deep gratitude to the Salvs, and sorrow.

Lums and Opians gathered along the Salv's trek to the ancient plateau to catch a glimpse of the Salvs. Some of them had never seen a real Salv in their life. Opian and Lum children clung to their parents tightly, more curious that afraid. The Luminist Masters gathered before the suspended Monoliths. The three Pyramids were inverted, level all around the exterior surface. There were no markings or indications of its origins, or manner of construction, no traces of any sort of entry point into the mysterious monoliths.

The inverted Pyramids were a luminous indigo and crimson and could be observed hundreds of Terran miles away. Junal and Seti assisted a very weak Master Seleyis in standing with his Yarite cane. Ojiri, Jodol, Lindra, Niris, and Jaanah stood around them. Juuri gazed at the titanic inverted Pyramids, suspended in the sky like indigo and red jewels. She could feel the surviving Salvs approaching over one hundred arci away.

Seti smiled as several Opian children ran forward, clearly belonging to Juuri's toola. The Opian and Lum crowds parted back several dozen meters as the Salvs somberly approached the plateau. Seti estimated there were less than three hundred Salvs. Nearly a hundred of them still suffered severe damage from the effect of the Red Vapor, unable to regenerate the damaged nerves and tissue until they entered the Pyramids. The crowd quieted as the Salvs slowly trekked up the desert plateau. Seti could see the remnants of the Seven leading the Salvs. Zevyla, Zilah, Zsiji, Zenobia, and Zephyra led the Salvs one hundred meters from the sacred Monoliths, suspended and luminescent in the Salv night.

Zsiji and her psimate Sapia led the Salvs in meditation as they all joined hands and their divis. The Salvs sat in silent meditation for several cycles, nearly fourteen Terran days.   Large numbers of the gazing crowd remained, but the majority of Opians and Lums returned to their Vils, to begin rebuilding and recovering from the aftermath of the Baali wars. Seti, Juuri, the Lum Masters, and their toolas remained and watched in silence. No one knew what the Salvs were going to do, whether they would simply disappear, or somehow enter the Floating Pyramids, or perhaps they would simply remain there in silence. Opians and Lums waited.

Suddenly, Seleyis started thumping his cane on the ground whispering yet no one could make out what he was saying. "Look!" Juuri whispered loudly. The Salvs began an elaborate ancient ritual, Salv skins flashed luminously from dark crimson to lighter tones, purple and blue highlights in long curving patterns appeared, disappeared, and reappeared. Their divi tentacles slid enjoined with each other, writhing and uncoiling, turning into patterns of alternating dark red, and violet.

The air became fluidic around them in the indigo haze reflected from the Febula Rings and Floating Pyramids. Glowing red meditation spheres formed around their bodies. The meditation spheres enveloped the Salvs. Hundreds of Salvs began melding and morphing into bizarre abstract forms, iridescent with all sorts of flashing colors.

The meditation spheres flashed brilliant crimson as dozens of them started to ascend, drifting towards the suspended Pyramids. A brilliant white and golden flash consumed each Salv meditation sphere approaching the exterior surface of the inverted wonders. Soon all the spheres disappeared into the Floating Pyramids with radiant white flashes. With each flash, a brilliant golden flame lingered on the surface where a meditation sphere disappeared.

Soon after the Salv meditations spheres disappeared in brilliant white and gold flashes, the Floating Pyramids were enflamed with a golden fire over most of its exterior. The golden flames of energy did not appear to damage the surface. Only six Salvs did not rise inside their meditation spheres. Zevyla, Zilah, Zsiji, Zenobia, Zephyra, and Sapia ended their melding meditations, dematerializing their glowing sphere. Sapia approached the Luminist Masters standing with Juuri and Seti.

The air was fluidic around Sapia and the Salvs. The Salv bioweb consciousness sang out in a resounding harmonic voice, echoing in the imaginary thought processes of the Lums. For the Lums, their minds felt the initial psychological wave of physical pleasure as their divis shuttered in bliss melding with Salv consciousness. Lum thoughts coalesced with Salv imaginative impulses. Atoms in motion unveiled alien conjunction in ethereal harmonics.

The Lost Planet is our home. Attempt no orbits or landings on the Lost Planet. Our past will become your future. One day Opians and Salvs will enter into a fellowship as trustees of the stars. The Time of the Sleep has come. Seti and Juuri smiled and freely shed tears, flashing their eyes after hearing Salvs telepathically repeat the message communicated to them in the biodomes.

Your civilization is violent and unsustainable. If the Opians do not foster evolutionary changes in your emotive impulses, your civilization will follow the course of so many others and destroy itself or expand into the universe with violent ambitions. The disembodied voices of the Lum Masters all seemed to speak at once due to their unnatural state of collective consciousness. *"Unforgivable... where will the Salvs go....some sort of transport?....remain on the Lost Planet?....in the debt of Salvs for generations...bio-plasmic bodies...never again will this happen .... unforgivable acts...."* The Salvs answered the confusing incomplete thoughts.

We have mastered quantum mnemonics, reverse engineering the bio-plasmic body or shadow matter of organic brains down to the neuronal or sub-neuronal level. Opian civilization must endure convergence on a civilization-wide social structure. Your civilization has no ecological harmonics or predictive ecological preservation. Your civilization has no maturing ingenuity in noetic sciences. You are not ready. These Monolithic containers were constructed by The Artisans. The Time of the Sleep cannot be delayed any longer; the regeneration of our procreative impulse must begin.

Seti spoke aloud. "Will we see you again?" *No precious ones. We will sleep for a long time. The universe has made us trustees of the stars.* The Luminist Ministers stepped forward with Seti and Juuri, and bowed reverently to the Sapia and the Salv emissaries. Sapia and Zsiji conjoined their divis with the other Salvs as indigo and red mediation spheres formed around the six Salvs.

The universe with sing with you as we dream. For the first time in over a thousand conjunctions,

Opians heard the audible voice of a Salv as Sapia spoke to them aloud. The glowing meditation spheres carried the Salvs high above to the suspended upside-down Pyramids. The Luminists watched with Juuri and Seti as the spheres disappeared in bright white flashes, adding more golden flames of energy to the Pyramids. The golden energy flames blazed and then dissipated. The three suspended Monoliths slowly changed color to crimson then indigo, silhouetted in the luminous blue misty haze that covered Planet Salv.

Inside the Pyramid Monoliths, the Salvs began the extensive regenerative process that would restore their damaged cells and instill the visionary procreative impulses they acquired from their nuptial rites with the Draags. Cocoons of fluidic white and golden light began to envelop each of the Salvs, laying in their biogenic units. Sapia and Zsiji watched as Zephyra, Zenobia, Zevyla, and Zilah entered their regenerative sleep.

Will we dream Zsiji? Sapia voiced her sister and mate. *Yes.* Zsiji answered. *We will dream. The universe will sing with us as we dream.* Sapia and Zsiji lay themselves into their biogenic units as their regenerative processes began. Across the universe, myriads of alien races lifted their heads, snouts, wings, orifices, tentacles, fins, and all sorts of appendages to the starry expanse…singing into the cosmic night for the trustees of the stars…

LOST PLANET

...

Until they awakened, the trustees of the stars did not know that the stars seen in their dreams did not exist. Stars fell around the Salvs. Minds reflected the deeps of space in violent loneliness. The Sleepers dreamt while The Artisans watched. *When the Trinity of the Watchers aligns in the skies of Salv, the Great Sleep will end…the floating Pyramids will upturn blackened as the cosmic night.* This was the Salv Prophecy foretold by the Salv oracle Zejiss at the Third Soliloquy of Convergence. The trustees of the stars awakened.

Inside the floating inverted monoliths, the latent Salvs lay encapsulated in a cocoon of fluidic white luminescence, which dimmed and dissipated as the Salvs awakened. Subconsciousness slipped into whirling reality as Sapia slowly opened her golden eyes. Psionic scans of her physiology revealed her body was quickly overcoming lasting effects of stasis and dystrophy. She could concentrate and regenerate the molecular cellular structure of her tissue within minutes; yet Sapia required all her psionic faculties in the Awakening.

The white luminescent cocoon dimmed around the surviving Salvs. Peering over to Zsiji's cocoon, Sapia could see the concern on her psi-mate's face as she regenerated damaged internal nervous systems. How many of them survived? Sapia could feel her psi-mates disquieting thoughts. Zsiji and Sapia slowly arose as white fluidic luminescence continued to dim and dissipate in succession, signifying awakening Salvs.

The luminous red and indigo floating Pyramids shuddered and slowly upturned. The floating monoliths now were proper crimson pyramids, shimmering red and indigo fluidic light. Slowly the luminous monoliths lost their light, dimming at first to a dull crimson, then turning hazy and opaque, finally to black. The Salvs inside quietly began to chant, first telepathically then as the psionic bond amplified, their psionic vital-force became aural. Harmonic conjunction lifted their chanting, echoing inside their monolithic Pyramids. Floating while suspended in the air, the blackened

Pyramids numbered three, resembling solemn death markers.

Inside the suspended black pyramids, the Salv chanting stopped. For many Salvs it was the first time they ever heard their own aural voices. Zsiji and Sapia moved toward the far wall of the Pyramid while the others telepathically voiced each other or reflected on hearing their own voices for the first time. Zsiji and Salv looked into each other's eyes, bonding telepathically as psi-mates. The two Salvs allowed the vital-force to flow into their divis, slowly sliding them and gyrating along each other.

Zsiji silently gave Sapia her affirmation within the telepathic bond. Sapia touched rhythmically a series of small oblong shapes near the centre of the far wall. A series of small glowing white lines appeared in succession and grew larger, creating geometric patterns the size of Salvs themselves. Sapia turned with Zsiji, their divis still undulating and intertwining slowly. She allowed her telepathic bond with Zsiji to encase each of the minds around her, feeling their thoughts and sensations. Each Salv reciprocated the psionic alignment, soon each felt the others neural pathways and pulsing divis.

Sapia spoke aurally; her melodic voice sang and resonated within the artificial Pyramids. *"Precious ones, the Great Sleep has come to an end. We are trustees to the stars; let us create a new alignment, as farmers in the fields of stars. Let us regenerate a new harvest and cultivate the breathing living deeps of space. We are patient but not immortal, we have so much to learn and harvest in this universe of a hundred billion galaxies, and other beings sing to us, the stars sang to us as we slept. Let us return the song."* Salvs began to chant telepathically and aurally reinforcing Zsiji and Sapia's psionic bond. Their vital-force caused glowing red mists to emit from their divis, morphing into radiant meditation spheres.

XXIII.   AWAKENING

The luminous red meditation spheres encased each chanting Salv, as their divis undulated and curled in harmonic conjunction. The Salv meditation spheres rose and hovered through the illuminated white geometric patterns on the blackened far wall. Setting down on the ground beneath the suspended Pyramids, the spheres dissipated as each Salv stepped out from within. Zsiji and Sapia looked at each other. The Salvs in their Pyramid were the only survivors. Sapia stood up from the meditation sphere and walked a few meters along the terrain of the Lost Planet.....

Sapia walked a few meters out onto the Fantastic Planet, which Salvs referred to since its ancient appearance in the skies of Planet Salv as the *"Lost"* Planet. Sapia stopped and gazed up at a monolithic statue of a humanoid head...

End.

PLANET SALV

by Joshua Seraphim

PLANET SALV

Leilah Publications